SUE BARTON: SENIOR NURSE

'I put you in on that case,' Miss Lester went on, 'because you can be very quick when you choose. Dr Reed is impatient and he won't have a slow nurse, no matter how good she is otherwise. I'd hoped that you –' She hesitated, and then said quietly, 'I'm sorry to have to tell you this, Miss Barton – but I find your work disappointing. When you first came to the Amphitheatre I thought you were going to be one of my best nurses. Instead, your work has been progressively worse. You're almost through here – and if there isn't an immediate improvement I shall not be able to send in a good report of you. Can't you keep your mind on what you are doing?

'I'll try,' Sue managed to say.

Other titles in the SUE BARTON
series are:

SUE BARTON: STUDENT NURSE
SUE BARTON: SENIOR NURSE
SUE BARTON: VISITING NURSE
SUE BARTON: RURAL NURSE
SUE BARTON: SUPERINTENDENT NURSE
SUE BARTON: NEIGHBOURHOOD NURSE
SUE BARTON: STAFF NURSE

Helen Dore Boylston

SUE BARTON: SENIOR NURSE

RED FOX

A Red Fox Book
Published by Random Century Children's Books
20 Vauxhall Bridge Road, London SW1V 2SA
A division of the Random Century Group Limited

London Melbourne Sydney Auckland
Johannesburg and agencies throughout the world

First published in Great Britain by
The Bodley Head Limited 1940

Text © Helen Dore Boylston 1937

Red Fox edition 1991

Set in Times New Roman by Speedset Ltd,
Ellesmere Port

Printed and bound in Great Britain by
Cox & Wyman Ltd, Reading

ISBN 0 09 975220 4

Contents

1	Senior Year Begins	1
2	Mystery of the Slips	14
3	Trouble on Ward 20	22
4	Operating at Last	34
5	Bill	51
6	Miss Meyers has Hysterics	60
7	Many a Slip	67
8	Mr Tait	73
9	Connie has an Adventure	88
10	The Christmas Eve Dance	95
11	A New Side of Life	109
12	Case Room	119
13	The Unexpected Always Happens	129
14	Another Shock	142
15	Last Months	148
16	New Plans	162
17	Graduation	171

1
Senior Year Begins

Brewster, the dormitory for probationers and junior nurses, stands on the outer fringe of the acres of hospital buildings, and that afternoon in September it was still with the stillness of an oven. The day nurses who were off duty were on the roof, stretched out in the shade of a great awning, where a wind from the river brought a suggestion of coolness. On the upper floors the night nurses slept in flushed restlessness, with doors and windows wide open to catch the least stirring of air. Downstairs, in the little tea-room at the end of the first-floor hallway, the sun crept under partly drawn shades and lay in blinding bars on the white tablecloth.

Norah, the little Irish maid, glanced wearily at the half-empty pitcher of iced tea, put down the nurse's cap she was making, and rose from behind the table. The sleeves of her black uniform clung damply around her arms, but her tiny white apron and ruffled collar were starched to a smoothness that no humidity could impress. She picked up the pitcher, stepped out into the hall, and disappeared down a flight of stairs beside an elevator shaft.

The deserted tea-room was so silent that the timid approach of two very new probationers had almost the effect of a flurry. They carried pens and large black notebooks which they placed gingerly on a chair, and then stood eyeing a plate of sandwiches on the table. The taller of the two was almost abnormally thin, with a sharp nose and pale, uncertain eyes. Her blue uniform hung lankly upon her. The other was short and pudgy and there was a dew of perspiration on her round face. The thin probationer spoke first.

'Maybe we better not, Mary,' she said. 'They might not like it.'

'Well, they won't miss one sandwich – and I'm starved.' She was extending a plump hand toward the plate when there was a step behind her. She jerked her hand back with guilty haste and turned, to encounter the amused eyes of a slender girl in the grey and white uniform of the student nurses.

The probationers looked at her with some apprehension. You never knew, in the hospital, *what* the nurses were going to say next. Still, this one seemed nice – not the teasing kind – and she was, as the probationers agreed later, 'the prettiest thing' they had ever seen. She stood easily, smiling at them, one hand buried deep in the pocket of her skirt. Her crinoline cap – so like an inverted teacup – rested on copper-red, soft curls. Her skin, except for a warm flush along the cheekbones, was transparently white, her features clean-cut and delicate.

'Aren't you having any tea?' she asked, in a clear, pleasant voice. 'Where *is* the tea, anyway? Goodness! People must have been gulping it down like boa constrictors!' She went to the stairs and called, 'Norah! Help! Tea!'

Norah's voice floated up the well of the stairway.

'Shure an' I'm comin'! Give a body time!'

The nurse laughed and returned to the probationers,

who had been watching her, envying her the grey uniform with its fitted bodice and full skirt, the starched white bib and apron that looked so business-like. But most of all, at that moment, they envied her her short sleeves and turn-over collar, open at the throat – for their uniforms had high collars, and long sleeves with five-inch, stiff cuffs.

'Have a sandwich,' the nurse said, offering them the plate.

The plump probationer's fingers closed on, not one, but three sandwiches, and the nurse grinned. 'I know just how you feel,' she said. 'But you'll get over being so ravenous after a while.'

'Is – is it all right,' the tall probationer asked, 'for *us* to have tea here?'

'Of course! It's for everybody. Didn't you know? And *do* sit down! It makes me hot just to look at you standing there in all those cuffs.' She added, explain-ing, 'You don't have to rise for older nurses when you're off duty, you know. I mean except for Sisters or Staff nurses.' She sat down herself, in a wicker chair by the table, and after an instant of shy hesitation the two probationers seated themselves side by side, prim in their blue and white. They were immensely flattered by her friendliness.

'Do you like it here?' she inquired politely.

'Oh, yes!' they chorused, and the lanky probation-er added surprisingly, 'It's so – so free here, isn't it?'

The nurse looked startled.

'What on earth do you mean?'

The probationer's heels twisted on the rung of her chair. 'Well, you see,' she began uncomfortably, 'at – at home – my stepfather was so strict. I couldn't ever do anything – or – have a minute to myself. He always wanted to know why I wasn't doing something different. But here – why, when I'm off duty I can do whatever I like – go out – or stay in – or read – or anything. And everybody is so – nice. I – guess you'll think I'm silly – but it seems like heaven to me!'

'Why, you poor lamb!' the nurse said gently, and the probationer flushed. 'I – this *is* a grand old place – though I must say I'd never thought of it as the last word in freedom. It –' she broke off at the sound of clinking ice behind her. 'Oh! Norah! Bless you!'

The little maid trudged across to the table, her movements heavy with the heat. But her face above the iced-tea pitcher was beaming.

'So – 'twas you callin', darlin'! 'Tis glad I am to see ye oncet more!' The tea was an amber stream into frosting glasses. 'Two sugars for ye – see – I'm rememberin'. Are ye afther likin' yer new room?'

The nurse's slender fingers closed gratefully on a cold glass. 'Yes,' she said. 'But I still feel like a stray cat over there.' She turned to the probationers. 'I just got back from the course in Eye and Ear Department,' she explained. 'And the Office put me in Grafton Hall – I'm the first of my class to move, and it's rather lonesome.'

'Yer friends will be follerin' ye soon enough,' Norah complained. 'Especially thim two young divils, Miss Halliday an' Miss Van Dyke. Ould Brewster'll be duller'n a back yard in th' rain, wid th' three of yez out of it.'

'Excuse me,' the stout probationer said, 'but are you a – *senior*?

'Yes – just. I've been a senior practically a week.'

'I – I thought you must be – if you'd been moved to Grafton Hall – because I know only seniors live there – but I've never seen you – I mean, why haven't we –'

'Why haven't you seen me around? Well, because I've been over at Eye and Ear Department, and before that I was on night duty, and before that I was at home recovering from an appendix.'

'Oh!' The probationer fell silent, overcome by the fact that she had actually been talking with a senior – who spoke of night duty as if it were nothing. The nurse sipped her tea absently, and after a few moments the probationer said timidly, 'Would you mind if I asked you something? We're so new here – and everything is so awfully confusing.'

The nurse looked up with an encouraging smile. 'Go right ahead.'

'Well – I don't understand about seniors. You said you'd been one only a week – but some of the nurses have been seniors longer than that, haven't they? How –'

'Why, you see, two classes enter the school each year. They come in six months apart. And each year, on the fifteenth of September, there is a graduation ceremony for both classes. They don't get their diplomas then, but they do wear the graduates' black band on their caps for that one night. Then they have to take it off again and wait until they have each put in exactly three years of work – to the minute. Lots of them have to make up time, too – on account of sickness or leaves of absence.'

'But –'

'There was a graduation just before you came, but hardly anybody actually graduated then. Mine is next

September – but I won't be through because I have two months to make up. In other words,' she smiled, 'there is one graduation ceremony a year, and the girls get through when they get through. Do you see?'

'Y – yes. Thank you.'

'Anything else?'

'N – no, I guess not – except –'

'Except what?'

'On – I was just wondering what it felt like to be a real senior.'

The nurse laughed understandingly. Then she sobered.

'It's not the way I thought it would be,' she said. 'I don't know exactly how to explain it. You're tired. You have a lot more responsibility – and you're two years older. I wouldn't say it's not as much fun – but it's a different kind of fun. That isn't very clear, but it's the best I can do.'

'Thank you very much.'

The thin probationer had been listening in a gloomy silence. The nurse turned to her. 'How are you making out with Miss Cameron, Miss – er – Miss –'

The girl started nervously, flushing again.

'Meyers – Annie Meyers,' she said in a low, self-conscious voice, and went on, speaking rapidly, 'I – I don't know how I'm getting on. I'm so scared of Miss Carmeron that I get all cold and clammy in her classes and can't remember anything – and she keeps telling me –'

'I know. She keeps telling all of us. We've all been through it. But Miss Cameron is a darling all the same. She's one of the grandest people in the world.

You may not think so now – but you will later.' She put down her glass and rose. 'Norah, are either of "thim two divils" around?'

'Sure – both of thim. They come over a bit ago – that's where all the tea wint.'

'I might have known! When you see a tea-table with that pathetic look of having been set upon by an army, it's always my little pals.' She nodded at the probationers, who had risen when she stood up, rested a friendly hand on Norah's shoulder for a moment, and then left the room with a quick, light step.

The probationers, following her with admiring eyes, saw her press the button for the elevator, and then stand reading the bulletin board on the wall. They heard her startled exclamation of '*Jiminy!*' The next instant she was flying up the stairs, regardless of the elevator.

The probationers turned eagerly to Norah.

'Who *is* she? She's lovely!'

'Ah!' said Norah. 'Didn't ye know? That's Miss Sue Barton.'

'*What?*' The word was a gasp from the thin probationer. 'You – you mean –'

'Not *the* Miss Barton!' cried the plump girl. 'The – the one they told us about in class – who saved a nurse's life – and the patient's, too – and got hurt doing it – because she was sick herself – I mean –'

'Shure – th' same!'

'But we've – been *talking* to her – just as if she was anybody! Why, if I'd known –'

'And she called me a lamb,' the thin probationer murmured in a dazed voice.

Upstairs on the fourth floor, Sue Barton, who had forgotten all about the probationers, was pushing open the heavy door that led to the roof. She knew that Constance Halliday and Katherine Van Dyke would be there. It wasn't necessary to look in their rooms. Everybody went to the roof on hot days.

The breeze from the river caught her full in the face as she stepped over the threshold and picked her way among the motionless forms on hammocks and cots to the far end of the roof. There were sleepy murmurs as she passed. 'Oh, it's Bat. Hello, Bat.' But not a head lifted. Beyond the awning, in the shadow of a bulkhead, two figures lay stretched out on a blanket, face down.

Sue dropped to her knees between them.

'Have you seen the bulletin board?' she demanded. There was a note of suppressed excitement in her voice.

Two heads turned simultaneously, and two pairs of eyes – brown and hazel – regarded her without the slightest interest.

'Certainly *not!*' said the prone figure with the hazel eyes. 'Why should we?'

'Go away,' muttered her companion, 'and take your bulletin board with you. We're sleeping.'

'Wait till you hear,' Sue said firmly. 'We're down for Operating Room Technique! But of course, if you want to sleep, the details can wait.' She rose to her feet. 'So long – see you to-night.'

'All right! You win! Wait, darn you!'

Both figures rolled over, wide awake now.

'Tell us!'

Sue beamed. 'The bulletin board is downstairs, on

your left from the elevator. Anybody'll show you.'
She went on in a half chant, 'Nurses should read the
bulletin board at least three times daily. It should
become a habit –'

'*Sue!*' The smaller of the two nurses was sitting
upright. 'You come back here!' Her hazel eyes, under
the shadow of heavy lashes, were startled, and the
clear, natural pallor of her skin was a shade whiter
than usual. The hand which pushed her straight dark
hair back from her face was not quite steady.

Sue was instantly sober. She dropped down on the
blanket again, glancing quickly from Connie to
Katherine Van Dyke, whose brown eyes were
interested but calm, and whose warm colouring,
made warmer by the rich brown of her hair and a
sprinkling of freckles across her nose, had not
changed. Her expression was slightly quizzical – but
the arch of Kit's eyebrows always gave her that look.
After her first surprised movement she had lain quiet,
hands clasped behind her head.

'It begins Monday from four to five,' Sue said.
'What *is* the matter, Connie?'

'That means we're – going to have operating –
almost at once!'

'Of course! What of it?' Kit said.

'What of it is that I'm scared to death,' Connie said
grimly.

'But *why*, Connie?' Sue was genuinely astonished.

'I – I don't know – exactly. I suppose – because I
don't think I'll be any good. I get worked up about
things – and operating is so – so sort of intense – and
you can't get rattled – and I will.'

'Nonsense!' Sue was brisk. 'You won't think twice

about it. You'll love it. I'm thrilled to fits. I've been waiting for it ever since I came in training.'

Connie lay back again with a nervous jerk. 'Wait till you get down in the Amphitheatre, and have to watch them opening up people! It's so unnatural and awful and –'

'Why is it?' Kit interrupted calmly. 'I mean – all sickness is unnatural if you're going to start thinking *that* way. Just let yourself go and you can work up an attack of horrors about a boil. Anybody'd think you'd never done a surgical dressing in your life!'

'Well, but –'

'But nothing! You've been reading the newspapers – and popular fiction – I know that stuff – "John Jones Goes under the Knife" – in great big headlines – and, "Great Surgeon Reveals What Goes on behind Closed Doors Where Muffled Figures Stand Waiting" – *phooey!*'

Sue laughed. 'Honestly, Connie, you're just dramatizing – you know you are.'

'Exactly!' Kit said. She turned on her side and looked at Connie seriously. 'Surgery's clean and quick – and one of the swellest things that has ever been done for human beings. *That's* dramatic – if you must have drama – and not all these bogeys about unnaturalness and gore and all that. What's got into you?'

'Oh, all right! I'm not scared if you say so,' Connie said, frustrated. Then, irrepressible to the last, she added, 'Aren't you scared at all, *honestly?*'

Kit considered this, staring up at a tuft of white cloud.

'No, I don't think I am,' she said at last. 'But I don't

know whether I'll like theatre work or not. It's one of those things you can't tell about.'

'I can tell about it,' Sue said. 'And I'm going to be good, operating, or break a leg trying. And I'm practically certain that I'm going in for theatre work when I graduate.'

Kit glanced at Connie, who grinned. An impish dimple appeared at the corner of Kit's mouth.

'Jove!' she said. 'You're jolly well steamed up, aren't you? Has Dr William Barry anything to do with all this enthusiasm?'

Sue flushed. 'Don't be so everlastingly British!' she exclaimed crossly. 'We all know you're a Canadian. We've known it for two years.'

Kit chuckled. 'Got you that time, didn't I? Well – has he?'

'No, he hasn't! I've *always* –'

'Here! Here!' Connie sat up again. 'Leave the poor girl her shy little secret. Whew! It's hot!' She wiped her small face with the towel that hung from her belt under her apron. 'We've got to be getting back on duty, Kitten. Are we sleeping up here to-night?'

'We certainly are!' Kit said, and Sue nodded agreement.

'Leave me the blanket,' she said. 'I'll bring it down.'

'All right; so long.'

The girls went away across the roof, back to the hot wards – Kit with her easy, swinging stride, Connie tiny and intense. The aprons glared for a moment in the sunlight by the door and then vanished.

Sue lay down on the blanket, yawned, and closed her eyes. The heat was smothering. She'd never be able to sleep. And what had Kit meant by that crack about Bill Barry? It was the first time she had ever tried to tease Sue about Bill – which meant that she had noticed something, some change, either in Sue herself, or in Bill.

And it couldn't be in herself, Sue thought, for she hadn't changed. She stirred uneasily and opened her eyes to stare up at the hot blue of the sky. It was Bill who was different. She might as well face it. Something disquieting had come into their very pleasant friendship – way back about the time when she had been a patient on Ward 3, and Bill had been her doctor. Anyway, that was when she first realized that he was changing.

He hadn't tried to see her any oftener after she left the ward and returned to duty. Their meetings were always chance encounters around the hospital, for student nurses were not allowed to go out with doctors. Lots of them did, of course, and it could have been arranged. But in the beginning their friendship hadn't been that kind – and now . . .

She turned again on the hot blanket, restless and pondering. Why try to keep their relationship on its old footing? She was terribly fond of Bill. There wasn't anybody else. And she certainly expected to fall in love and marry, some day.

'But not now!' she thought desperately. 'Please, not now. I'm – I'm *busy!*'

High overhead, wisps of cloud hung in the blue. The heat waves quivered over the roofs. Under the awning the occasional low drone of conversation sounded like the bees around the porch vines at home. Sue's long lashes dropped to the curve of her cheek, and slowly the fingers of the hand she had flung out on the blanket began to relax. Darkness crept across her mind. She slept.

2
Mystery of the Slips

Operating Room Technique Three was, as its name indicated, the third class of its kind.

The first came during probation and taught the principles of asepsis, or, as Sue, who was then unaccustomed to medical terms, expressed it, 'free from germs, and why couldn't they just say so and let it go at that?' The probationers were given instructions for 'the scrub', each in turn having to scrub hands and arms up to the elbows with soapy water and a brush. This made the hands 'surgically clean' but not sterile, and they must next be plunged into a strong antiseptic solution. After that, the probationers put on a sterile gown and struggled into rubber gloves.

Dressed in this strange and uncomfortable garb, they were taught to use sterile forceps for moving all sterile instruments or supplies. They must never, the instructor assured them, touch the points of the instruments, for hands were never perfectly sterile, and even rubber gloves were not as easily sterilized as metal. They learned how to unfold sterile gowns, towels, and sponges, and discovered through bitter experience that things which were to be kept sterile must never touch anything unsterile. Dry goods were the only exception to this. One side of a sheet or towel could be unsterile, and the other side, if not wet, would remain sterile unless it came in direct contact with something 'dirty.'

The second class came during the junior term and dealt with the preparation of patients for operation, and with their care afterwards.

The third class, beginning now, in Sue's last year, she found a little disappointing, until the final lesson, for it was an intensive review of the already familiar aseptic procedure. But in the final lesson they were taught how to make the supplies and drains used in the Amphitheatre itself, and they watched with intense interest while the instructor 'set up' a nurse's table for a simple appendix operation.

'This is only to give you a general idea of methods,' she told them. 'I don't expect you to remember the details. The arrangement of the tables will be taught you in the Amphitheatre.'

The girls filed out of class feeling that they were about to take part in world-shaking events. The only question was – when? For only a few of the class would go to the Amphitheatre at one time.

The question was not answered for several days, and in the meantime fall classes began – senior classes in medical and surgical emergencies, in neurology and psychiatry, in nutrition, in the nursing care of maternity cases, in public-health nursing, and in ethics.

In addition to this and their work on the wards, Sue's class, by ones and twos, began to move to Grafton Hall. It was the day that Connie was moving that an odd thing happened – mere chance, it seemed, at the time.

Sue and Kit had been helping to carry Connie's

various belongings from Brewster to Grafton Hall, and they were returning for another armful apiece. As they passed the door of Miss Cameron's suite on the first floor of Brewster, Sue had an impulse.

'Come on!' she said to the girls. 'Now we're leaving Brewster for good we ought to go in and give Miss Cameron kind of a "hail and farewell." '

'Not me!' Kit said. 'I'm just as scared of her now as I was when I was a probe. I'd as soon go to the electric chair as walk through that door. You two go – I'll wait here.'

'My apron isn't very clean,' Connie said hastily. 'I'll wait with you. Go on, Sue! Hurry up!'

They hovered gingerly in the corridor while Sue approached Miss Cameron's door. Sue was nervous herself, now, but her mind was made up.

The door stood open, the room only partly concealed by a screen, and Sue caught a glimpse of the impressive figure in white, sitting like a ramrod before a small writing desk. Miss Cameron dominated the room as she dominated everything. Her official position was that of instructor in practical nursing and supervisor of Brewster. Her jurisdiction over the girls ended, theoretically, with their probation. Actually it never ended. Once you had been Miss Cameron's pupil you were her child always – to be scolded lavishly and praised with restraint. The nurses loved, reverenced, and feared her.

In response to Sue's tap an abrupt voice said, 'Come!'

Sue went around the screen.

Miss Cameron looked up with the expression of a traffic officer confronting a hit-and-run driver. Then her mouth unclamped in a warm smile.

'Well – Miss Barton! This is very nice. Come right in, child, and sit down.'

'Thank you, Miss Cameron, but I can't stop. I'm helping Miss Halliday move to Grafton, and I have to go back on duty in a few minutes. But I saw your door open – and I thought –' Sue paused, intensely aware of Miss Cameron's eyes missing no detail of face or clothing.

The eyes softened. 'I see. It was good of you to stop and visit me. What are you doing now?'

'I'm on Ward 20, Miss Cameron, and I'm – at least, I *think* I'm going to work in the Theatre, soon.'

'Operating? Already?'

'But I'm a senior now, Miss Cameron, and –'

'So you are! So you are! Well, you will have to give proper attention to details in the Amphitheatre. It will be good for you.' There was a pause. Then, 'Are you eating as you should?' The question came with disconcerting suddenness.

'Yes, Miss Cameron.'

You don't look it! You're much too thin! I shall speak to the Office about you! A special diet –'

'I'm all right, Miss Cameron, really I am,' Sue protested.

Miss Cameron promptly disposed of the protest.

'Young people to-day have no judgment about themselves – none whatever – running around looking like starveling white mice –' She broke off, her eyes on the hem of Sue's skirt, towards the back. '*Is that your slip showing?*'

Sue flushed and tried to see the back of her skirt, not daring to mention the fact that she had no slip on.

'I – I don't think so, Miss Cameron.'

'Well, something shows! You mustn't be careless about your appearance. We can't have that in our young women! And it isn't like you, Miss Barton.'

'I'm very sorry, Miss Cameron.'

Miss Cameron glared. Then she said more gently, 'There, child, I won't scold you. But don't fidget! If you must go, go along. I know you have a great deal to do. Run along now – *but fix that slip at once!*'

'Y – yes, Miss Cameron,' Sue stammered, and fled.

'Whew!' she said to the girls when they were out of earshot of Miss Cameron's room. 'I adore her – but it's sort of like calling on a machine gun. And for goodness' sake,' she added, 'will you look at the back of my skirt and see what's showing? She said it was my slip – but since I haven't one on, it –'

'It serves you right,' Kit said with a grin. 'You would go in there – and you know what she's like.'

'Nothing's showing,' said Connie, who had dropped back to look.

'What do you suppose she saw?'

'Goodness knows!'

The girls wondered briefly about the mystery and then forgot it, intent on getting Connie settled in her new room at Grafton.

It is probable that they would never have thought of the matter again if it hadn't been for the probationer encountered in the hospital subway a few days later.

The basement of the hospital was a vast honeycomb of underground passages connecting every building in the institution, and offering many short cuts to hurrying nurses and doctors. Sue and Kit were returning from a class in neurology. They had taken a passage-way that led past the basement of Brewster, where, long ago, Sue had been so hopelessly lost, and had been rescued by Dr Barry.

As they went by the entrance a probationer emerged with a strained expression on her face. This was too usual with probationers to cause comment, but this one's behaviour was anything but usual. She contorted her entire body in an effort, it seemed, to look down her own back, first from one side and then from the other. She hadn't seen the approach of the girls and her gymnastics took up the whole passage-way.

'Here! Here!' Kit said. 'What's all this? Is it a game, or are you trying to reduce?'

The probationer untangled herself with a jerk of surprise and embarrassment.

'I beg your pardon,' she stammered. 'I didn't – see you. I – Miss Cameron just told me my slip showed, but I can't seem to see it, and –'

'It doesn't,' Sue assured her. 'Really it doesn't.'

'Oh – th – thank you!' The probationer hurried away, leaving the girls staring at each other.

'What goes on?' Sue demanded.

'Search me!' Kit shrugged. 'Maybe Miss Cameron ought to be psycho-analyzed.'

'But why slips? I mean, why not pink elephants on the wall, or a spook following her?'

'Well, I can't answer for elephants, but I assure you, my lamb, that no spook would dare follow Miss Cameron – even at night, in a cemetery, with all his friends around!'

Sue laughed and the next instant was startled to see Kit vanishing through an adjacent door with the remark, 'Here comes your Hero. See you later!'

'Wait, Kitty!'

But Kit was gone.

Sue was annoyed. Why did people – even Kit – have to put that kind of construction on things? Her annoyance was forgotten, however, as she watched the tall young doctor coming towards her and thought that he was really very distinguished-looking, with his fine head and loose-jointed grace.

'Hello, Sue Barton!' he greeted her warmly. 'Where have you been keeping yourself?'

'Hello, Bill!' Sue was frankly glad to see him. 'Up on the medical wards.'

He leaned back against the wall, hands deep in his hip pockets, and looked down at her with his grave, pleasant eyes.

'Seems to me you're having a good deal of medical duty. You must be a senior now. Oughtn't you to be having operating before long?'

'Yes. As a matter of fact I think it will be very soon, though I'm not sure – there are so many of us.'

'I'll be glad when you do,' he said simply. 'I've – missed seeing you.'

Sue changed the subject hastily.

'In the Amphitheatre,' she said, 'will you have to call me *Miss* Barton?'

'Certainly not!' he said, laughing. 'The Amphitheatre is, in its way, the most informal place in the hospital, I shall call you Sue – unless, of course you'd like to be addressed as "Hey, you." It would sound well, don't you think?' He tried it. '*Hey*, you! Hey, *you!*'

'I like the first one better – it's a little more general. But I don't intend to answer to either. Besides, I'll probably be too unnerved there to notice you.'

'You won't be unnerved in the Amphitheatre. You'll like it, I hope.'

'I'm sure I'll like it. I've looked forward to it all through training, and if I'm good I think it's what I want to do when I graduate.'

'Oh,' he said. Then, 'You're grimly determined, I suppose, to have a career?'

'But of course! What did you –' She broke off hastily and glanced at her watch. 'Goodness! I've got to be back on duty or Miss Martel will have a stroke.' She paused, and then said in a mock-tragic and sepulchral voice, 'Good-bye, Bill!' Her eyes were bright with mischief teasing him.

'You're a brat!' he exclaimed, half laughing. 'I ought to shake you!'

'And,' Sue thought a few moments later as she watched his white-clad figure disappearing in the distance, 'he'd be perfectly capable of doing it, too.' She grinned suddenly. 'But he'd better not!' she said aloud.

3
Trouble on Ward 20

It began with Tony, the laundryman.

Oddly enough, it was Tony who had been responsible for Sue's friendship with Bill Barry. If she had not fled from Tony in a blind panic her very first day in the hospital, when she had been lost in the subway, she would never really have known Bill. At least, not in the same way.

Tony's disposition, as Sue remarked once to Connie, was always even – 'just one continuous fit of rage.' He had been so violent without cause that day in the subway, when she had asked him the way out, that she had run for her life. And Bill Barry, an interne then, had come upon her, sitting on a steam pipe and quite hysterical. Under these informal circumstances their friendship had its beginning. It was Bill who had come to her, who had remained with her, the night she had her appendix out. Sue was the first person he had told of his appointment as resident surgeon to the hospital.

They had been real friends, and they had always said that it was Tony's fault. More than once, when Sue had chanced to meet Bill in some corridor, they had seen Tony's lumbering bulk and walrus moustaches in the distance, and the corridor had echoed with their remembering laughter.

Now it was Tony again.

Sue and Kit were both on duty on Ward 20, a women's medical ward in the old part of the hospital. The wards there were inconvenient, but Sue loved them. They had a Victorian air, with their fireplaces and their uneven floors. Ivy, planted long ago, crept over the stone window-sills. The squares of sunlight on brown linoleum and white beds seemed the sunlight of other years. Rainy days on Ward 20 made Sue think of attics and old trunks. The busy small sounds that were a part of the day's work – the clink of dishes in the kitchen, the rattle of the dumb-waiter, the scratching of the head nurse's pen, the clean rustle of fresh sheets, the low murmur of patients' voices – all seemed quieter and more leisurely than in any other part of the hospital.

Sue would have been happy there if she had not disliked her head nurse. This was unusual. Sue's first head nurse, Miss Waring, was still her friend and adviser. Her other head nurses, with one or two exceptions had been women with humour, imagination, and efficiency.

Miss Martel was reasonably efficient, Sue supposed. At least, the work on the ward got done as well as elsewhere. But Miss Martel was not blessed with humour and her imagination had taken the wrong turning. She was a small, sallow young woman with perpetually angry eyes, who took offence at almost everything the nurses said or did.

'She acts,' Kit said bitterly, 'as if we were caterpillars – and she didn't like bugs.'

The week of the crisis with Tony, Sue was laundry nurse. Twice a day – before ten-thirty in the morning, and before four in the afternoon – she had to empty the laundry bags and go through the contents in search of stray drinking tubes, safety-pins, rubber sheets, and other miscellany which had no place in the laundry. Once she had actually found a huge irrigation can entangled with a sheet. 'Though how anybody got it there without hard labour I can't imagine,' she complained to Kit.

When the process of research was ended the laundry was stuffed back in the bags, which were tied at the top and tagged with the name of the ward and of the laundry nurse.

The newer hospital wards had laundry chutes, but the old building had none, and to save time and labour the bags were dropped out of the laboratory window which opened on the well of the staircase. They had a clear fall of three stories to the basement – where they were picked up by Tony and his handcart.

Tony was not the only laundryman, but he was the only one who made an impression on the nurses. He had worked in the hospital for fifteen years – in a state of chronic fury – and his close-cropped black hair, choleric face, and bristling moustaches were only too well known.

'How he survives it is a miracle,' Sue had remarked only that morning. 'He's so massively fat to be so frantic. I'll bet his blood pressure is sky high!'

'Well, do hurry!' Miss Martel snapped behind her. 'It's late now and you'll have him up here, raging. I've asked you over and over again, Miss Barton, to have the laundry ready on time.'

'But, Miss Martel,' said Sue, reasonably, 'I started out here to do the laundry once before, and you asked me to go to the dispensary. I'm awfully sorry I was so long, but I couldn't help it. The prescription wasn't quite ready.'

'You always have an excuse, don't you, Miss Barton?'

'But it was your own –' Sue bit her lip and fell silent.

'Just what were you going to accuse me of, Miss Barton?'

'Nothing, Miss Martel.'

There was a step behind them. Miss Martel turned sharply. 'What are *you* doing here, Miss Van Dyke?'

'Why – uh –' Kit was genuinely bewildered. 'I – I came out to get a drinking straw for Mrs Finnegan. Shouldn't I?'

Miss Martel's eyes narrowed. 'There was no need to creep out like that.'

When the little head nurse had stalked away Kit turned on Sue.

'For Pete's sake!' she exclaimed. 'What's the matter with her now?'

'Gee, I don't know. She hasn't had a spell as bad as this in ages – not since the time Ted Hanscom dropped the patient's false teeth down the sluice, and Martel got the notion Ted did it on purpose.'

'If you ask me, I think Martel's got delusions of persecution, or something.'

'I'm sure she has – but I don't know what we can do about it.'

The girls went on with the work, feeling more uneasy than usual – which was saying a good deal, for there was never any knowing what form Miss Martel's tantrums would take.

The staff nurse, however, seemed to have given sufficient vent to her ill temper for the present, and the girls got through the morning and part of the afternoon without any further trouble which could be termed definite. She sat stiffly at the desk, her smouldering eyes watching everything that went on, but she made no comment.

'She doesn't have to!' Ted Hanscom said to Sue. 'All she has to do to get me rattled is to sit there and follow me with those eyes.'

'Do you suppose the Office knows the way she is?'

'They can't! They'd fire her,' Ted said with simple faith.

It didn't occur to either of the girls that there was another possibility – that the Office might be aware of Miss Martel's peculiarities and was giving her a chance to overcome them.

'You know, Barton,' Ted went on, 'I think she's got an extra down on you and Van. You'd better look out, or she'll make trouble for you.'

'I *am* looking out,' Sue replied grimly, 'and that's all the good it does me! I'd give anything to get off this ward.'

And so the girls grumbled when occasion offered, and worked with one eye on Miss Martel.

'Honestly,' Kit said out of the corner of her mouth as Sue passed her with a medicine tray, 'I'm practically hysterical. If she doesn't stop that looking, I'll scream.'

'You needn't think that will get you off the ward. There's not a chance!'

'You're telling me!'

The afternoon wore on. Several patients were transferred to other wards. New patients were admitted. It was late again when Sue hurried out to the laboratory to do the laundry, forgetting in her nervousness that she had left a basin of soapy water on a bedside table – where Miss Martel could see it. Miss Martel was rigid about the nurses leaving equipment around. This was true of most head nurses, but they were usually reasonable about it, and made allowances.

Sue found three partly filled laundry bags open on the racks by the laboratory window. Two others, already full, leaned against the wall. Sue emptied these last, went through the laundry rapidly, replaced it, and tagged the bags. She was just beginning on the racks when, through the open window above the stairs, she heard a grumbling roar.

Tony was on his way up!

Kit, who was making a bed near the ward door, heard the roar and came out.

'I'll help you,' she said, grinning, and seized a bag.

Tony's lumbering steps and heavy panting grew louder. He muttered hoarsely as he climbed.

'Martel will be wild if he gets up here!' Sue picked up a finished bag and dropped it out of the window. 'Maybe that'll stop him!'

But the steps came on, and the muttering increased as the bag struck the basement floor, three stories down.

Sue leaned out of the window and tried once more.

'Wait, Tony!' she called, pleading. 'They're coming right down.'

Tony's reply was an unintelligible howl which Sue prayed was not heard by Miss Martel in the ward. She could see his overalled figure on a bend in the stairs, clambering upwards, his short black hair bristling on his bullet head, his moustaches straight out, his fat arms waving.

Two more bags were ready by the time Tony reached the top of the last flight of stairs, charged through the door, and around the corner into the laboratory. His face was purple and he hissed, shaking his fist in Sue's face. Then he pounced on the laundry bags.

He snatched the last one off the rack without waiting for it to be sorted, threw it out, seized another that stood against the wall. The girls were helpless.

Tony swooped up a full bag. It was unusually heavy and he swung it back once, experimentally. Then he took a firmer grip on it, wheezing at the girls over his shoulder.

Miss Martel came round the corner.

Her face was grim and accusing, and she was carrying Sue's basin of soapy water.

It all happened in an instant.

The heavy laundry bag came back and upward with a vicious swing, caught the tiny head nurse in the region of her diaphragm, and lifted her clear off the floor. The basin of water flew toward the ceiling, turned over, and fell. Its contents landed squarely on Miss Martel's cap at the precise moment when she hit the floor – sitting.

There was a moment of hideous silence.

Tony's eyes bulged. Then he strode across Miss Martel's extended legs and fled.

Miss Martel sat, struggling for breath. Her cap was crushed flat. Water dripped from her hair and ran down the front of her white uniform in soapy bubbles. Her eyes were glassy with the shock of the blow.

Sue and Kit stared, equally stunned. Then the tension, which had been increasing steadily since morning, snapped suddenly and completely, catching both girls unprepared. Their faces quivered.

Laughter, incredible and shocking, came upon them.

It welled in their throats in a rising tide of hysteria. They rocked back and forth, limp and helpless. Their hands made feeble gestures. They gasped and choked, clutching one another for support, sank slowly to the floor. There was a pain of laughter in Sue's chest. She could neither speak nor move, but leaned against the shaking Kit.

Through the fog of their uncontrollable mirth they were dimly aware that Miss Martel had recovered her breath, that her white face was turning crimson. Her voice came at last.

'*Get up!*' she shrilled. 'Get up and help me!'

The girls looked at her feebly, quite literally unable to stir. Tears poured from their brimming eyes. Kit drew a long crowing breath. Sue could make no sound at all, though her mouth opened.

Somehow, Miss Martel got to her feet and reached mechanically to touch her cap. Her fingers encountered the sodden pancake and at the expression of sheer fury on her face both girls collapsed utterly.

The little nurse turned without another word and went straight through the linen closet to the telephone.

The girls, from the floor, heard her shaking voice through their whimpers of laughter.

'Training School Office, please. . . . This is Ward 20, Miss Martel speaking. . . . I'm sending Nurse

Barton and Nurse Van Dyke to the Office. . . . Yes, at once. . . . For impertinence and insubordination. . . . Yes, very. . . . Thank you. . . .'

Even this terrifying development had no immediate effect. The girls were by this time nearer to tears than they knew – tears of embarrassment, regret, and fear. But nothing stopped their laughter, nothing came to relax the strange force which had clutched them.

They managed to stagger to their feet by the time Miss Martel returned.

'We – we're – frightfully sorry –' Sue gasped. 'We – didn't mean – *truly* –'

'*Go to the Training School Office at once – both of you!*'

'Y-yes, Miss Martel,' Sue choked, and then, in spite of all her efforts, went into another fit of laughter.

All the way to the Office, down long flights of stairs, through corridors, the girls fought to stop the spasms that overcame them. They progressed with contorted faces and a strange weaving motion.

At the entrance to the big rotunda in the Administration Building they paused and leaned against a wall. The telephone operator glanced at them over her black, horn-shaped mouthpiece and began to laugh herself.

'What's the joke?' she said.

'It – it – isn't – a joke,' Sue whimpered.

'I see; just practising for a funeral, I suppose.'

'Practically that,' Kit said feebly. 'What'll we do, Sue?'

Sue made another effort.

'J-just look at that door – over there – a minute. The sight of – it – ought to fix us.'

It did, for 'that door' was the door of the Training School Office. The girls fixed their eyes on it, and the realization of what would happen to them, once they were over its threshold, had a definitely subduing effect.

Presently Kit said, 'I'm all right now – I think. Are you?'

'I – guess so. Come on! Off with our heads!'

They were quite sober as they crossed the great airy rotunda and approached the fateful doorway.

'Every last supervisor is there,' Kit said in a low voice. 'They would be!'

Four icy pairs of eyes greeted them, travelled slowly over their uniforms, and returned to their faces. Sue glanced at Miss Mason, the elderly assistant superintendent, who was noted for her kindness and understanding. Miss Mason returned the glance with one which froze Sue to the marrow.

'Will you tell us at once, please,' Miss Mason said, 'what has happened!'

There was an instant of silence. The four supervisors waited motionless behind their desks. Then Kit spoke.

'We're terribly sorry, Miss Mason. We didn't mean to be' – a slight tremor shook her – 'insubordinate – or – impertinent. It was an accident.'

'Yes?' Miss Mason's voice was ominously calm.

'It was like this,' Sue put in – 'Tony, the laundry-man –' She told the story, a little haltingly, but clearly, omitting any mention of the strain to which Miss Martel had subjected them all day. If the keen professional eyes of the supervisors noted symptoms of latent hysteria they gave no sign of it. When Sue came to the description of Miss Martel reaching for the sodden pancake that had been her cap, there was a faint sound from one of the younger supervisors – a choking sound which hurriedly became a cough. Miss Mason's lips quivered, and reset in firm lines. Her eyes, which had been fixed on Sue's face, dropped quickly. When they lifted again they were utterly without expression.

Sue continued. 'And so,' she finished at last, 'when Miss Martel told us to help her – we – we couldn't. Honestly, Miss Mason – we weren't able. It – it was dreadful – and we're awfully sorry. We wouldn't have acted like that on purpose for anything in the world.'

There was another silence.

Miss Mason said slowly, 'I think that it would be advisable, Miss Barton, to separate you and Miss Van Dyke. You will report to Ward 8 for duty immediately. But before you go, you will return to Ward 20 and apologize to Miss Martel.' She turned to Kit. 'You also, Miss Van Dyke. I am sending you to Ward 19. You will explain to Miss Martel that I am sending her some other nurses at once. It is shocking that I should have to removed two *seniors* from a ward for such childish behaviour. I hope that there will never be occasion for me to do so again as long as either of you is in the school. *Is that clear?*'

'Yes, Miss Mason.'

'Very well. You may go.'

'Thank you, Miss Mason.'

The girls wheeled with decorous precision and went out, across the rotunda. As they reached the corridor

Sue thought that she heard a sound of laughter – almost an outburst. But she wasn't quite sure. The sound was smothered immediately.

Kit performed a brief tap step.

'Whoops!' she chortled. 'Isn't Mason an old darling? I believe she caught on to all we didn't tell her!'

'Of course she did! Don't be an idiot!'

'Well, are we in disgrace, or aren't we?'

'Naturally we are! But do you realize that we have escaped from Martel?'

'Have we ever! And trust Ma Mason to fix it, too!'

4
Operating at Last

It was Sue's transfer to Ward 8 which was to involve her once more in the matter of Miss Cameron and the slips – but not immediately. A great deal was to happen before that minor affair assumed any importance.

Sue liked Ward 8, though the work was harder than on Ward 20, for the majority of the patients were seriously ill. Miss Hendricks, the stout, capable, and talkative head nurse, welcomed Sue cordially, and thereafter left her to do her work in her own way.

There was nothing in the world, Sue thought, as absorbing as a really sick patient. They needed everything she had to give – skill, inexhaustible sympathy, and understanding. She loved the long ward with its sun-room, its rows of white doorways, its cheerful kitchen, its busyness. But most of all she loved the patients, yearned over their helplessness, rejoiced in their improvement.

'I'd never make a good private nurse,' she thought more than once, 'One patient isn't enough. I like lots and lots of them around, and heaps of equipment to work with.'

The satisfaction of Ward 8, however was somewhat dimmed by the prospect of operating, which might become a reality at any time – for there was a rumour that some of the new seniors were to be sent to the Amphitheatre very shortly.

Sue gave baths, made beds, in a fog of daydreams, seeing herself in the Amphitheatre. There would never before have been such an operating nurse! She and Kit, and Connie, of course – but here Sue's dreams failed her, because, for the first time, Connie didn't fit into the picture.

It was natural, Sue supposed, that as imaginative and high-strung a person as Connie should be in a dither about operating. Lots of the girls were very nervous when they first went to the Amphitheatre, but nobody, except the ones who were scared, paid any attention to it. Connie's case, however, was a little different.

In the first place, she hadn't said a word about operating since that day on the roof when she had admitted being afraid and when Connie was unduly silent she was likely to be working up to something.

'She just can't go to pieces in the Amphitheatre,' Sue confided to Kit. 'It would spoil everything.'

Kit agreed gloomily, for Sue's last remark had been a reference to Connie's early difficulties in the school. She had arrived with a handicap. The nurses had heard that Connie's father was both wealthy and socially prominent in Chicago, and they were sincerely convinced that no 'rich society girl' would take a nurse's training seriously, or stand up under its strain.

Sue's loyal protests that Connie wasn't a bit like that had no effect, and she didn't feel at liberty to explain that Connie had been unhappy at home, that her mother didn't like her, and that Connie had come to the hospital as to a haven after the uproar caused by her refusal to marry the man selected for her by her mother.

It was Connie herself who by slow degrees had proved the nurses' estimate of her mistaken. They had accepted her at last as one of themselves, and Connie had been very proud of that triumph.

'All the same,' Sue thought, 'if she gets the jitters in the Amphitheatre they'll go right back to their first idea. They'll say they were right after all, and she's falling down on the job when it comes to anything hard – as if being here and doing good work for two years weren't enough proof that she's all right. And she's so sensitive it'll just about kill her if they turn on her like that.'

Somehow Connie's horror of operations must be concealed until she had time to get over it. But how? Sue couldn't think of any way.

A day or two later Sue was laying out her clean sheets for the morning's bed-making when the telephone rang. Before she could put down her armful of linen the head nurse's voice announced:

"Ward 8, Miss Hendricks speaking. . . . Certainly. . . . At once. . . .' The receiver clicked.

Miss Hendricks rustled into the linen closet.

'Oh, there you are, Miss Barton! The T.S.O. has just called. I'm afraid I'm going to lose you. I'm so sorry. I'd intended –'

Sue put down the pile of sheets.

'– They said they were sending me another nurse, but I do wish they'd make these changes later in the day – of course, in your case it had to be now – but they *could* have sent the other nurse yesterday afternoon so she'd have had time to get used to the ward, instead of the first thing this morning, with all the work piling up –'

'Excuse me, Miss Hendricks,' Sue interrupted in desperation. 'You didn't say where I was going –'

'What? Oh, goodness! Didn't I? Why, you're to report to the Amphitheatre at once, and –'

'*The Amphitheatre!*' Sue's heart turned completely over.

'Yes. Of course, you'll be on call from here, but it isn't likely that you'll be back here any day until way in the afternoon, just about in time to take temperatures –' The head nurse paused and smiled at Sue. 'I do run on, don't I?' she said. 'I expect you ought to go. Good luck, Miss Barton.'

'Thank you.' Sue hurried down the long corridor to the door. Her hand was damp on the knob, and there was a tightness in her chest, but her steps were light along the old brick corridor that led to the Amphitheatre – and to the beginning of the work she had waited for, for so long. If she were lucky, Kit would be there to work with her – and Connie. Sue quickened her pace. Nothing must happen to Connie!

The brass-plated doors of the Amphitheatre gleamed before her in the darkness of a turning.

Sue halted abruptly – hesitated. Then she placed a resolute palm against the brass. The doors opened on sudden, complete whiteness, on a winter of corridors and tiled doorways; and closed in a gust of hot air, sickish with ether and heavy with the brown smell of scorching cotton.

Sue swallowed the pricking in her throat, resisted an impulse to sneeze, and went on, trying to seem gaily nonchalant – for at the end of the white tunnel of corridor three familiar figures watched her approach. An arm lifted in greeting and Sue waved in response.

The three new operating nurses stood awkwardly around the Amphitheatre supervisor's desk – Connie, Hilda Grayson, and Lois Wilmont. Sue moaned inwardly at the sight of Lois. For two months or more they would have to have Lois around – 'Willie,' with her long nose, her prim mouth, her too neat sandy hair, and her self-righteousness. She'd be good at operating, too. That was the worst of it.

Fat, pretty Hilda, of course, was a darling. She was no intellectual giant, but she was sweet.

'Hello!' the three chorused.

'Hello,' Sue returned. 'Well – here we are! And I'll bet nobody can think of a more obvious remark than that.' Sue was laughing, but she cast an anxious glance at Connie, whose manner was composed, but whose lips were white. Sue put a steadying hand on her shoulder. 'Who do I report to?' she demanded ungrammatically of Lois.

Lois, for once, let the question of grammar pass unnoticed.

'You report to Miss Lee, the supervisor,' she said. 'She's been called away for a few minutes. We're to wait for her here.'

'Thanks.' Sue turned to Connie. 'Where's Kit?'

'She isn't coming,' Connie said faintly. 'We're all there are this time.'

'Well, we can't have everything, I suppose –' Sue's voice trailed off. She thought, 'Connie's *terribly* scared! What'll I *do* with her – without Kit to help? And I can't talk to Connie about it right here in front of everybody.'

There was a silence. The four girls stood looking about them, trying to fit themselves into the new background by sheer force of attention. Sue was eager; Connie pale and resigned; Hilda awed. Lois was the only one who seemed entirely sure of herself. 'And she's faking,' Sue thought, glancing at her. 'That expression is too lofty to be real.'

The small rotunda where the girls were waiting was the centre of the great labyrinth of whiteness, the heart of an incessant, quiet stir of preparation. Nurses came and went, in operating gowns and the nunlike headpieces, their feet whispering on the white mosaic of the floor. Brown-clad orderlies appeared and disappeared. House officers erupted through doors to a sound of running water and the hiss of steam.

'It's all so interesting!' Sue thought. 'I don't see why Connie is so scared. Anyway, she's bound to get over it soon.'

But Connie's eyes were dark with terror watching an anæsthetist trundle past wheeling a fantastic clump of tanks and balloons.

Sue's mind, in spite of her anxiety about Connie, wandered to Bill Barry. She could scarcely not think of him, here in his own domain. This was his world. He was important in it. She wondered if he knew that she had come to the Amphitheatre. He was anxious to have her here, she was certain. He wanted to show her how important he was – dear Bill. Sue smiled wistfully. If only he wouldn't sort of hurry her, perhaps. . . And that was odd, too. Because he didn't do or say anything to try to make her respond to him. It was all inside him – a kind of tense waiting.

Two house officers paused at the desk to make suitable, grinning comment on the new operating nurses, and then went on. Sue, coming out of her

thoughts with guilty haste, was relieved to see that the
house officers' gay impudence had distracted Connie
for a moment – had taken her out of herself. And a
minute later there appeared the graceful, sauntering
figure of Dr George Alexander Lamson, senior house
officer, with his waxed blond moustache, his chal-
lenging eye for a pretty nurse, his caressing manner
for the elderly or plain.

'Oops!' Connie murmured at Sue's shoulder, in
quite her normal voice. 'Does he come with the
course, or is he extra, like fancy dancing?'

'Extra,' said Sue. 'Imported by the management at
terrific expense.'

Dr Lamson smiled into Hilda's dazzled eyes,
breathed on Lois, patted Connie on the shoulder, and
then stood back to look at Sue.

'Well, well, and *well*!' His eyes darkened deliber-
ately.

Sue laughed.

'Go away!' she said. 'You frighten me!'

The voice of Miss Lee, the supervisor, spoke
behind them, a firm and pleasant voice, as amused as
her eyes.

'Shoo, George!' she said. 'We don't want you!'
Then, to the girls, 'pay no attention to him or he'll be
as thick around as a swarm of bees.'

'You flatter me –' Dr Lamson was beginning, when
a masculine voice in the distance called, 'Hey!
Lamson!' and he retreated, with a final liquid glance
over his shoulder at Sue.

Miss Lee picked up a paper from the desk.

'I'll be with you in just a minute,' she said, and
hurried away, young, attractive, and incredible calm.

'*Really!*' Lois remarked. 'This seems to be a very casual sort of place. I must say I'm surprised.'

'Why don't you suggest some improvements to Miss Lee?' Sue drawled. 'That ought to create a little tension.'

Lois checked her reply as an operating nurse hurried up to them, her expression worried.

'Wasn't Dr Lamson here just now?' she asked breathlessly.

'Why, yes, he was,' Sue replied.

'Well, would one of you find him and ask him where the neck tourniquet is – for the thyroid case?'

'*I* will,' Lois said promptly.

'Thank you so much – and hurry!'

Sue choked and Connie's lips quivered. Lois favoured them with a glare apiece and hurried away. The operating nurse grinned and retreated to a doorway.

'W-what is it?' Hilda asked, bewildered.

'Shhh! It's an old joke, darling. They always try it on new nurses.'

'But –'

'Look, Hilda,' Connie said gently – more colour returning to her face as she spoke. 'You aren't thinking, lamb. What would happen to a patient if you put a tourniquet around his neck – and pulled it tight?'

'Why – *oh!*' Light dawned in Hilda's round eyes. 'Why – he'd choke to death! I see now! There isn't any such thing as a neck tourniquet. You'd think anybody would see through that, wouldn't you?'

Sue kept a straight face. 'Yes, you would, but lots don't, I expect, or they wouldn't keep trying it.'

'What do you think is going to happen?'

'I don't know,' Connie said. 'Wait and see.'

They waited. Connie seemed all right now. The nonsense appeared to have restored her to an ordinary state of mind.

Lois presently emerged from somewhere and hurried towards them. Dr Lamson's head appeared around a door casing. His face was one broad grin.

'He thinks the orderly took it!' Lois said in an expasperated voice as she passed them.

They watched her go from the orderly to the sterilizing room, dash out again, and engage a desperately unsmiling anæsthetist in conversation. Then her tall, prim figure vanished through yet another door.

Connie took a step forward.

'Look here,' she said, 'I think we're being mean. We're just as new as Willie, and she isn't a bad sort underneath. I hate them all to laugh at her – and I'm going to tell her before she makes any more of an idiot of herself!'

To Sue's amazement Connie went quickly along the white corridor after Lois, turned in at the same doorway – and came out again precipitately. Her face was as white as the wall.

'A – a house officer – is doing – an operation – in there!' she gasped.

'*Connie!*' Sue's voice was sharp. '*Stop that!* You must! Do you hear?'

Connie gripped the corner of Miss Lee's desk.

'I'm all right,' she said after a moment. 'Don't worry. I – I'll snap out of this in a minute.'

Sue turned to Hilda, who was staring, wide-eyed.

'Hilda! You keep still about this! It doesn't mean a thing. Connie hasn't been feeling well lately, and –'

'Why of course, Sue. I – I wouldn't dream –'

She was interrupted by Lois, who stalked up to them, her face burning.

'You knew all the time!' she accused them. 'I think you might have told me! This isn't the place for silly jokes. I – what's the matter with *you*, Halliday?'

Sue held her breath.

Connie said quietly, 'Nothing whatever.'

Sue breathed again.

'Well,' Lois went on, 'naturally I should have seen it was a joke anywhere but here. In a place like *this* it didn't occur to me that –'

'Are you ready, girls?' said Miss Lee beside them.

They followed her on a tour of inspection, through the white corridors: into the gleaming, hissing sterilizing room with its acrid smell of hot cloth; through the instrument room, walled with glass cabinets; into the tiny anæsthetic rooms with their sweet, sickish smell.

Miss Lee explained, pointed out, asked them to remember this and that; finished at last with everything external to the operating room and announced:

'If you will come with me, now, we will go through some of the operating rooms.'

Sue looked quickly at Connie. She was still pretty white. But she *had* been feeling better, and perhaps, if they didn't go through that room from which Connie had returned so hysterically, she might still pull herself together.

Miss Lee's capable back moved on before them, through a series of deserted operating rooms. Everything was neat, and white, and exactly the same in each room. Miss Lee's pleasant voice directed the girls' attention here and there. Sue was beginning to feel easier about Connie, and breathed a sigh of relief when Miss Lee remarked that it would not be necessary to go through all the operating rooms at the moment. They were alike in their arrangement, as the girls had seen, and there wouldn't be time, now, to see them all. The girls must watch the setting up of tables.

'I am going to turn you over to the head nurse, Miss Lester, now. She will explain the duties of an operating nurse. There won't be much for you to do to-day, except learn the arrangement of the nurses' tables. When Miss Lester has finished with you, you will watch a simple operation for a chronic appendix, and then you may return to your wards for the day.'

They were to watch an appendectomy! A cold chill ran down Sue's spine. Connie was in for it now! There was no escape. 'Oh, what'll I do with her?' There was nothing she, or anyone, could do. It was up to Connie alone. She'd always been brave and fine. Surely now, at the last moment, her courage would come to her rescue.

Sue listened to Miss Lester with only half her mind. The ability to concentrate which two years of training had given her enabled her to absorb the lecture. She heard Miss Lester saying that they must have a thorough knowledge of the steps of any operation so that they might anticipate the surgeon's needs; that they must not speak to the operating surgeon unless he spoke to them; that the nurses' tables, with needles, sutures, ties, and sponges, were always set up in the same way. This was so that any nurse could 'take over' the table and know where to find each thing.

The crisp voice went on, and the one half of Sue's mind listened and remembered. The other half circled wearily around Connie. She mustn't make a mess of this. She'd be quite capable of leaving the hospital, if she did make a mess of operating – and the hospital meant more to Connie than to most of the nurses. It had given her something real, and vital – something to work for, to be a part of. If, now, she felt that she had failed it – 'Oh, no!' Sue moaned inwardly. 'Oh, Connie! Try! Try hard!'

A door behind them opened and a nurse came in to say that the appendectomy was about to begin.

Miss Lester rose, nodding to the girls. They followed her in complete silence.

Connie's lips were a quivering line. As the girls entered the operating room and climbed onto the little brass-railed observation stand her eyes dilated – enormously. Sue caught her hand. It was ice-cold.

'Connie, *darling!*' she whispered. 'Don't!'

There was no reply.

On Sue's other side Hilda and Willie sat rigid, on the edge of their seats.

Two gowned operating nurses appeared in the doorway wheeling their sheeted table. An orderly followed with the stretcher bearing the profoundly sleeping patient. An anæsthetist hurried beside him, pulling after her the gas-oxygen machine.

'Nervous?' Hilda whispered to Sue.

'No – are you?'

'Nope! I've been down here quite a few times – and then I was in the Throat Room.'

'Same here.'

Connie sat like one carved from stone.

A house officer appeared and pushed his table of instruments into place. And then the tall figure of the surgeon, bare hands and arms dripping soapy water down his white trousers, came briskly though the doorway.

It was Bill Barry.

His eyes met Sue's in a second of shock. Then he turned away to plunge his hands into a jar of alcohol. Miss Lee hurried to help him with his gown. A nurse held his gloves. The orderly tied on his mask. What they did was routine, but the way in which they did it impressed Sue more than anything that Bill himself could have said or done. 'It's almost as if he were one of the staff men,' she thought 'I'd no idea he was so important.'

Dr Barry looked up at the row of grey and white uniforms in the observation stand.

'Well,' he said lightly, 'this is very nice!' His eyes twinkled over his mask. 'Four brand-new nurses for an audience.' He turned to the anæsthetist. 'Patient all right?'

'Yes, sir.'

The operating nurses had been laying sterile towels over the patient's abdomen, leaving exposed a little square of iodine-painted skin.

Dr Barry picked up the tiny, glinting knife.

Connie's hands closed on the brass railing before her. Her mouth opened in a faint gasp. Sue heard it and moved closer until their shoulders touched.

There was a quick, sure movement of the gloved hand holding the little knife, and a white line ran thread-like down the centre of the painted skin. Sue waited for the towels to stain red, pressing her shoulder tight against Connie's – but no red stain appeared. The gloved hands were too quick, clamping and tying off the tiny veins and arteries.

Dr Barry began to talk, explaining what he was doing, and in the pauses when he was silent, his eyes intent on the movements of his hands, Miss Lester murmured to the girls, calling their attention to the work of the operating nurses.

'At this point,' Dr Barry said, 'I use carbolic crystals for cauterization –'

Sue felt a stir against her shoulder and turned her head quickly. Connie was swaying. Her eyes were closed and her lips were blue.

Sue's hand closed on the arm beside her with a grip of iron – a cruel and painful grip, but it brought Connie back for a moment, and her lips parted in a shallow gasp.

Dr Barry glanced up. His eyes caught Sue's look of desperate appeal and went to Connie's face. Miss Lester was watching the operation. She had not noticed Connie. Dr Barry hesitated. Then he said clearly, 'Oh – Miss Halliday – you're right next to those shelves. Would you take down that jar of zero catgut, please, and bring it here? This stuff is heavy enough to moor a liner.'

Both operating nurses looked up, briefly astonished; but they were resigned to the vagaries of surgeons and after their first surprise went on with their work. Miss Lester, pleased that Dr Barry was encouraging one of the new nurses to take some small part in the proceedings, made no attempt to get the jar herself, and smiled at the young surgeon.

Sue relaxed her hold on Connie, who rose heavily and fumbled among the jars, taking – thank goodness – the right one. She stepped down to the floor holding the jar in an unsteady hand.

'Just bring it here,' Dr Barry said. 'Now take the cover off. That's right.' He smiled at Miss Lester – the smile of one instructor to another. 'Thank you.' He dipped into the jar with his forceps and drew out two coils of catgut, one of which, apparently by accident, fell to the floor. 'Sorry,' he murmured, 'Just lay it back on the shelf. It can be resterilized.'

Connie stooped blindly and Sue, watching, saw that bending over had brought a little colour back into her face. Her limp fingers found the catgut and placed it on the glass shelf beside her. When she straightened up her eyes had lost their blank look, and Sue breathed an inward blessing on Bill. How quick he'd been to see, and to do the right thing! Two years of training had given Connie the habit of instant, unquestioning obedience. A doctor needed something. Connie's fading consciousness told her that she must get it. The effort had restored her somewhat, and bending over had brought the blood back to her head. Bill was a darling!

'You're so small, Nurse Halliday,' he was saying in his pleasant voice, 'that I'm sure you can't see well from the stand. If you'd like to stay here I can show you better what I am doing.'

'Th – thank you,' Connie whispered.

Sue was startled. This wasn't so very bright of him. If Connie had to stay there she'd faint all over again. But Sue had reckoned without Bill.

He was speaking again, directly to Connie, his

voice compelling her attention. His deep-set blue eyes, shadowed by the rim of the mask, looked up from time to time, to hold Connie's gaze. Sue had always known that Bill could talk well when he was in the mood to do so, but she had never heard him as eloquent as now. His words dropped, one by one, into Connie's mind, stripping surgery of its horror and its dread; revealing it as an exquisite skill, a precise pattern of healing.

And Connie listened, reluctantly at first, then with growing interest.

When he turned to the anæsthetist and said, 'Keep him under a little longer, please,' Connie looked up involuntarily.

'Did you want to ask me something?' he said.

Connie nodded.

'I thought the breathing was supposed to change when a patient needs more ether,' she said in her normal voice. 'I – I didn't see that it had changed.'

His eyes smiled approval and Connie flushed.

'The breathing does change,' he said. 'But sometimes, before the change in respiration is noticeable, there is a slight stiffening of the abdominal muscles.' He added casually, 'Would you like to see?'

There was a pause. Then, to Sue's amazement and delight, Connie stepped forward – very careful, as she had been taught, not to brush against anything – and peered into the incision. The colour which had come back into her face remained there, unchanged. Her eyes were clear – interested.

She was looking at an operation – at last – in terms of impersonal mechanics.

Sue leaned back in a glow of gratitude for Bill, of

admiration for Connie's pluck, and watched the quick, smooth finish of the appendectomy.

Connie would be all right.

'And maybe now,' Sue thought, '*I* can begin to learn something about operating.'

5
Bill

Before Sue returned to Ward 8 for the day she went in search of Bill. Somebody, she thought, ought to thank him for what he had done for Connie. He had left the operating room, after the appendectomy, before Sue had an opportunity to speak to him – and now she felt a little shy about doing so.

Bill in the rôle of surgeon was almost a stranger – a detached and brilliant stranger. The attitude of the operating nurses had added to this impression.

'And who am I,' thought Sue, half amused and half in earnest, 'to speak to so much grandeur?' But she spoke to him, nevertheless, catching him just as he was leaving the Amphitheatre.

'Bill – wait!' she called, hurrying down the white corridor.

He turned quickly, smiling his grave smile.

'Hello, what's the rush?' he asked. Without the grotesque garments of the operating room he was just Bill again.

'I wanted to say something to you,' she said, coming up to him, breathless. 'I – wanted to thank you – about Connie.'

'Oh,' he dismissed the matter easily, 'that's all right – the poor kid.'

'It was splendid of you!' Sue looked up at him with so clear and sweet a gaze that he caught his breath.

'But you – you mustn't think,' she went on, 'that Connie's a coward. She's the bravest person I know. It's just that she has more imagination than most, and –'

'Of course!' he said heartily. 'It never occurred to me to think her a coward. I think she has an extraordinary amount of courage. It takes that, you know, to go on when one is afraid. You'd understand that – you've rather a lot of courage yourself.'

'I?' Sue stared at him.

'Yes, you. What about the nurse whose life you saved on Ward 3?'

'But that was different. I didn't have time to think. If I had –' She paused, drawing a sharp breath. For a second she saw again the patient's delirious eyes close to hers, saw the darting hand reaching for the little bedside table – and shuddered.

'Sue! My dear–' Barry said tenderly. 'I – I didn't mean to –'

'Hope I'm not interrupting anything,' said Dr Lamson's voice. They turned.

'Oh, it's you, George,' Barry said.

'As far as I know – it's me,' Lamson said cheerfully. He touched his moustache with a reverent hand and smiled at Sue. 'Fascinating view of the corridor wall, isn't it?' he went on.

His complacency irritated Sue.

'Perhaps we could arrange a different view for you,' she said crossly. 'How about a nice mirror hung there, where you could look into it?'

Lamson was undisturbed. His brown eyes wandered over Sue's hair, then turned to Barry, whose face was slightly red.

'I like the child,' Lamson said. 'She tried so hard to be cutting, and only succeeds in being charming. Don't you think she's charming, Barry?'

Sue laughed – a laugh which meant only that she thought Lamson rather silly; but Bill misunderstood. His eyes hardened.

'Yes!' he said through his teeth, and without another word he nodded briefly at Sue and stalked from the Amphitheatre.

Lamson stared after him.

'Whee!' he said. 'What's the matter with our little boy? Somebody take away his playthings?'

'I think he's tired,' Sue answered quietly, but she had been startled and, in spite of herself, a little amused. She didn't want to be amused at Bill in that way – but he *had* been rather like a furious small boy.

She went on to Ward 8 feeling that she knew very little about managing men, and that as a result Bill was becoming more and more difficult. And he was such a dear, really, if only he'd be content to leave things as they were. Lamson she forgot at once.

Her worry that Bill might continue in this present disagreeable mood seemed to be groundless, however. For the next day he was quite as usual – friendly, charming, and busy about his work.

Sue found that working in the Amphitheatre was not so different, after all. No matter where one was in the hospital there was always routine, and one quickly became a part of it. Every morning on the ward the telephone rang and there was a request that Miss Barton come to the Amphitheatre. Every morning when Sue arrived there she read the list of the day's operations and, after the fourth day, scrubbed and helped to set up tables.

At the end of the first week she was allowed to 'go in' on a minor operation, as assistant to one of the experienced nurses. She had very little to do. There were a few packages of sponges to open; she held an instrument or two for the operating house officer, was unable to see what he was doing, had her toes stepped on, and stood around feeling unnecessary. It was a little disappointing; but that, she told herself, was because she wasn't far enough advanced in the work.

'I'm *going* to be crazy about it, I know!' she told the envious Kit.

'I'm crazy about it already,' Connie said happily.

Connie was doing splendidly in the Amphitheatre. She had no more attacks of jitters, and Miss Lester had been heard to say that little Miss Halliday was amazingly quick. Sue noticed that Connie lingered in the Amphitheatre when the day's work was finished, and that she was frequently to be found talking with the anæsthetist. Once, passing an anæsthetic room, Sue caught a glimpse of Connie poring over the various gadgets on the gas-oxygen machine.

'It was almost as big as she was,' Sue reported to Kit that night. They were curled up on Sue's bed, as usual. Nurses seldom stand when they can sit, or sit when they can lie down.

Kit laughed. 'How's our Willie? she asked idly.

'Oh, Willie's perfect, of course. And you should *see* Hilda. She goes around simply bulging – eyes and all. But she's such a good kid, and she tries so hard; everybody likes her.'

Kit sighed. 'I wish I were there. I like the wards, but after two years you get sort of tired of them.'

'Well, you'll be along pretty soon,' Sue returned absently.

'My! You mustn't let yourself get worked up about it like that. Hey! Are you listening to me?'

Sue came back with a start. 'Of course I'm listening to you. I heard every word you said.'

'What was the last thing I said?'

'Oh – er – why, you said you were sort of tired of the wards.'

'Ha!' said Kit triumphantly. 'You *weren't* listening. What were you thinking about?'

'Oh, nothing special – this and that.'

But Sue had been thinking, and very uneasily, of something that had happened that afternoon. The day had been rainy, and for once Sue disliked the thought of returning to the ward. It would seen dreary, she thought, after the warmth and whiteness of the Amphitheatre, and she had offered to stay on and help the operating seniors, who had no ward duty, their job being to keep everything up to scratch in the Amphitheatre.

Miss Lee had been pleased, and presently Sue found herself alone in one of the operating rooms, wiping off glass shelves and tidying up generally. Through the closed door to the sterilizing room she could hear the sound of mopping and of smothered laughter, and gathered that Annie, the big sterilizer, had overflowed again.

The operating room was warm and white and quiet. Sue finished the shelves in a little glow of contentment and turned to survey the room. It was about finished.

But one of the glass-topped instrument tables had been left standing askew in the middle of the room. Sue crossed to it, to push it back against the wall, when a childish impulse seized her. She gave the table a push, flung herself upon its glass top, and rode smoothly and silently across the room, to bring up with a thump against the wall, under the big window.

'How about a nice box of blocks – or maybe a kiddie car?' said a laughing masculine voice.

Sue scrambled off the table, feeling foolish.

'Oh – hello, Bill!' she said.

'Hello,' he returned softly.

The light from the vast window fell clearly on his tall figure, on his young face and tired eyes.

'All in?' Sue asked gently.

'Yes – a bit.'

'I'm so sorry.'

'Thanks.'

There was a companionable silence. He was too tired, to-day, to be difficult, Sue thought, relieved. They stood side by side, looking out of the window, their elbows resting on the narrow sill. Sue cupped her chin in her hands and stared at the rain, slanting silver against the red brick of an opposite ward. Through the ward windows she could see the nurses busy about their work; the stout maid doing dishes in the kitchen; the patients warm and safe in their beds, and listening to the cold drip of rain outside.

'It's a pretty grand old place, isn't it?' Bill said at last.

'Yes.' Sue paused, and then went on musingly, 'But you know, here in the Amphitheatre I miss the patients. You never get to know them – and they're so dear and – and foolish, and exasperating.'

'You like people, don't you?' he said, looking down at her.

'Very much.'

'So do I. It's –' he was beginning, when a nurse put her head in at the door.

'Oh, George!' she called. And then, 'Oh – sorry, Dr Barry. I thought you were George Lamson.' She vanished.

Barry's face was crimson. He stared out of the window, saying nothing, his lips a thin line.

Sue stole a glance at him. Then she said quietly, 'You don't like Dr Lamson very much, do you?'

He was silent a moment. Then he turned and looked at her, standing slim and straight before him.

'Not particularly,' he said. 'Do you?'

'Why – I don't know. I hadn't thought. He's a harmless, amiable soul.'

'I wish you'd tell me,' he said slowly, 'why girls like that type of man. Because they do like him – and you know it!'

Sue considered, chin in the palm of a slender hand. 'I don't know, exactly,' she said 'He's entertaining – and he sort of flatters our vanity, and –'

He drew a quick, sharp breath. 'I didn't think,' he said harshly, 'that you were the kind who cared for cheap, insincere flattery, but apparently you do. I noticed the other day –'

'Bill!' Sue had straightened up, her eyes blazing. 'That's absolutely uncalled for – and besides, it's none of your business.'

'I beg your pardon,' he said sulkily.

There was a silence. Sue got herself in hand. They couldn't go on like this. It was absurd.

'Let's not quarrel, Bill,' she said. 'It isn't worth it.'

His eyes softened. 'I know,' he said. 'It was rotten of me.' He held out his hand. 'Am I forgiven?'

'Of course!' Her hand clasped his, and suddenly they laughed. When their laughter died away reaction left them silent again.

Then Barry said, smiling, 'You do like me a little – still, don't you?'

'I can bear you,' said Sue lightly, 'I even admire you – sometimes – though I'm sure it's presumptuous of me, when there are so many and better nurses to worship at your feet.'

He grinned. 'I was hoping you'd noticed that!'

'Dear me, how you do hate yourself! And would you kindly tell me what you think you've got – except your elegant black hair? Where would you be if you were bald – or even if it were rumpled? All women would flee from you.'

'You might rumple it, and find out if you want to run,' he said, bending over. His dark head was very close – a well-set head on broad shoulders.

'No, indeed,' hastily. 'I wouldn't dream of it.' She was laughing a little.

He straightened up. 'Why not?'

An odd sensation, almost like fear, stirred within her. 'I – I don't know,' she said, and looked up at him with eyes in which there was no trace of laughter.

There was a silence.

Then Sue turned back to the window.

'Look,' she said, a little unsteadily, 'the lights are on in the ward now. In a little while the girls will be getting out the supper trays. It's strange, isn't it, to think how many years that has been going on? The people come and go, but they're just the same, really.'

'Yes,' he agreed, watching her.

They talked for a few minutes: of the hospital; of the work that was being done in the laboratories on pernicious anæmia; of the difference between medicine and surgery. But when Barry went away at last, Sue remained, staring out of the window with a troubled face, until Miss Lee came to find her, and say that everything was done and she had better return to the ward.

6
Miss Meyers has Hysterics

Sue had very little time, however, for meditating on her state of mind and emotions – or on Bill's. The hospital was too demanding.

In the Amphitheatre, by the end of another week, she was allowed to be first assistant to one of the senior house officers who was doing a chronic appendix. The operation took exactly fifteen minutes. Sue knew every step of it by heart, and everything went off smoothly – for she had exerted every possible effort to that end. Afterward, thinking it over, it seemed to her that her part in the operation had been very slight. Surely there must be more to operating that this. It wasn't, she felt, that it was easy. One had to be alert every moment. That was just the trouble. One had to do beautifully and with great care and attention something which, as part of the whole, was very important, but which by itself was – Sue hated to use the word – dull. It couldn't be that, surely – not operating – when she'd wanted it for so long.

Back on Ward 8 in the evenings, both the Amphitheatre and the problem of Bill vanished from her mind in her absorption in the patients and their needs. There were medicines to give, tired backs to rub, supper trays to get out. In addition there was Annie Meyers, the lanky probationer with whom Sue had talked that hot day in the tea-room of Brewster.

Miss Meyers had been on duty on Ward 8 for several days, and the nurses were beginning to wonder about the girl, and to discuss her among themselves. She started when spoken to, moped in the linen closet, and flitted in and out of the patient's rooms like a distracted ghost. Sue, always warmly sympathetic, began to be seriously worried about the probationer and tried to draw her out – with no result. Miss Meyers seemed to be in a state of humble, incoherent worship of Sue, and could only stare at her dumbly, muttering replies to Sue's kindly questions.

It is possible that the nervousness of Miss Meyers would never have been explained if it had not been for an entirely irrelevant circumstances – a sudden desire of Connie's, one evening, to make fudge.

Kit had been out to the little store on the corner to buy the necessary ingredients, and on her return the girls descended to the kitchenette – only to find that other nurses had been seized with a similar idea, and there was no room on the stove, or in the kitchenette.

'Let's go over to Brewster,' Connie suggested. 'Maybe nobody's using the kitchen there.'

Nobody was.

The fudge had been bubbling briskly for some time, and the girls were testing a drop of it in a cup of cold water when, without warning, the intent silence was broken by a sob. They turned sharply and peered out into the dinette, to see a lanky figure in blue standing by a window, staring out.

'It's Annie Meyers,' Sue whispered.

The probationer was obviously unaware of their presence, for her thin back had the slumped, defence-

less look of a person who believes herself alone. Her
shoulders quivered.

'What's the matter, Miss Meyers?' Sue called after
a moment. 'Can I do anything?'

The girl whirled about, and then made a pitiful
effort to seem casual. 'Why – er –' she began. Then
her weak smile faded and her face crumpled.

'Oh, M – Miss Barton!' she wailed, and dropping
into the nearest chair buried her face in her arms and
sobbed aloud.

Sue hurried across the room and put a hand on the
probationer's bony shoulder. Kit and Connie remained discreetly in the kitchenette doorway.

'Couldn't you tell me?' Sue asked. 'I've seen for
some time that something was the matter and – I
hoped you'd let me help you.'

The probationer tried to rise but sank down under
the pressure of Sue's hand.

'I – I wish I were dead!' she moaned. And then,
with mounting hysteria, 'I w-wish I'd never – b-been
b –'

'Stop that!' Sue's voice was crisp. 'Nothing's as bad
as all that. Here, sit up and tell me about it. I'm sure it
would make you feel better.'

The sudden authority in Sue's tone got results. Miss
Meyers made an effort, pulled herself upright, and
raised a pair of blurred, red-rimmed eyes to Sue's
face.

'I'm s-sorry,' she quavered. 'I didn't – know –
anybody was here. It – it's been dreadful!' Her face
crumpled again and Sue's grip on her shoulder
tightened. 'I – I've never been any good at anything,'
she faltered. 'I'm so – scared of everything – I haven't

any – push to me. E-even Mother says so. But I did –
so want – to be a nurse. And if – if she sends me home
– now – I'll die. I couldn't *bear* –' her voice was
growing shrill again.

'Who wants to send you home?'

'M – Miss Cameron!'

'*Miss Cameron!*' Sue exclaimed. 'Just a minute –
what, exactly, did Miss Cameron say to you?'

The girl's swollen eyes filled again.

'She said I – was a disgrace – to the school. She
s-said I ought to be home – with my mother – b-because
girls who were – careless how they l-looked oughtn't
to be – nurses. She said there were – already – too
many like that – and the – the hospital better – get rid
of them!'

'I don't see anything the matter with the way you
look,' said Sue, lying tactfully. 'And you mustn't get
worked up over the things Miss Cameron says. She
talks like that to everybody, and she doesn't mean it
at all. Underneath she's a darling – she's one of the
kindest, fairest people in the world.'

'B-but she *said* –'

'It doesn't matter what she said. She hasn't the
faintest idea of sending you home. What did she think
was wrong with you?'

'She – told me – my slip showed. She told me –
e-every time I came in her r-room. And when I l-looked
I couldn't ever see it, so she said to-night – that if – I
couldn't keep – my clothes on I'd better – go home.'

Sue exchanged a look with the girls in the doorway.

'See here,' she said to Miss Meyers, 'there's
something funny about this –'

'It isn't – funny to me.'

'Cheer up – maybe it will be after a while. Anyway, Miss Cameron told me the same thing.'

'*You*, Miss Barton? Oh – she *wouldn't* –'

'Wouldn't she! And she's been accusing people all over the place of losing their underwear. It isn't reasonable. I didn't even have a slip on, the day she told me mine showed. So you see you aren't the only one, by any means. Cheer up, now!'

'But – she s-seems to feel sort of strongly about me, and –'

'Nonsense!' Sue stood for a moment, thinking. Then she brightened. 'I'll tell you what,' she said, 'suppose you go and round up a few of your class who have had the same experience, and all of you go together to Miss Cameron, and tell her –'

'*Go to Miss Cameron?*' The probationer's eyes went glassy with horror.

'Surely. Why not? Listen –' Sue pulled up a chair and sat down. 'You've got a lot more spunk than you think you have. I don't believe you're really so timid – if you were, you would never have screwed yourself up to come in training. Now you're here you want to get something out of it – and you can't if you go around cringing all the time. Miss Cameron won't bite you. And there's something odd about all this slip business.'

'I – I couldn't ever go to Miss Cameron on p-purpose.'

'Yes, you can. You'll be doing something for all of us if you find out what the fuss is about.'

'But how *can* I?'

'Well, that's up to you, isn't it? You can figure out what to do when you get there. You won't be alone, you know, if you take some of the other girls who have had the same trouble with Miss Cameron.'

'I – couldn't; please don't ask me to.'

'But I am asking you to,' Sue said firmly.

'S-she'll eat me alive!'

'No she won't. She'll like you for coming to her about it. And I'll promise you something – if this doesn't turn out all right, I'll go to Miss Cameron myself, and explain about you.'

'You'd – do that – for *me!*'

'Of course!' Sue was on the verge of saying that she would do as much for anyone in such a state, but thought better of it as she saw the dawn of something like determination in the probationer's face.

Miss Meyers' awed, humble eyes were fixed on Sue's face. After a long time she said slowly, 'I – I'll try – if you want me to, Miss Barton. I guess – things couldn't be any worse than they are.'

'Good girl!' Sue rose, and Miss Meyers stood up, wobbly but faintly resolute.

'You've been *wonderful*, Miss Barton! I – I don't know how to thank you. If I – get through this – you'll have done it –'

'I'll have done nothing of the sort. You're doing this, and don't you forget it!'

'But you *have* been wonderful, Miss Barton. Thank you so much.' The lanky, tearful figure stumbled from the room and a moment later they heard her uncertain step on the stairs.

'Gosh, Sue!' Connie said from the doorway. 'Do you suppose she'll do it?'

'I don't know. I hope so.'

'My, my!' said Kit, grinning wickedly. 'Wonderful,

wonderful Miss Barton! Why not order up a cage of wildcats for the girl? She'd get in with them if you wanted her to – and they'd be simple after bearding Miss Cameron in her den.'

'Sue's right, though,' Connie put in. 'If Meyers once gets over the idea that she's a mouse she might be quite a person. And she has to start sometime – if ever. Miss Cameron will do for her to cut her teeth on.'

'Break her teeth on, you mean!' said Kit. 'Simple Susie the Sunshine Girl! Mother's little helper!' She turned to the amused Connie. 'Oh! Are you there, Miss Halliday? Excuse me for not seeing you – but I was so dazzled –'

She laughed and went on into the kitchenette.

The fudge, long neglected, was badly overcooked. The girls looked at it unhappily. 'And a nice mess,' Kit grumbled. 'All on account of your charitable instincts, Sue. Look at it! It's going to be as hard as granite.'

'I wonder,' Connie mused, 'if she really will do it.'

'If she does,' Sue returned, 'we'll hear about it. It'll be all over the hospital by morning. Anyway, what I want to know is – what about those slips?'

'Well, you'll probably hear about that, too.'

And they did.

7
Many a Slip

Sue barely got to breakfast on time that morning. She never minded getting up early in summer, but now that year was well into November and the mornings were frosty, it was hard work to crawl out of her warm bed.

She dashed through the dining-room door just as it was closing, took her napkin from its pigeonhole, and looked across at the table where her 'crowd' always sat. Kit and Connie and Lois Wilmont were already there, and Hilda Grayson was just ahead of Sue, with her tray.

Sue reached the table just as Hilda was sitting down. There were sleepy good-mornings, except from Hilda, who seemed unusually bright and wide-awake.

'What do you think has happened?' Hilda began at once.

'I know,' Kit said solemnly, looking up from her cereal.

Hilda's face clouded. 'Do you? What?'

'Miss Mason has been secretly married to the head orderly for five years, and he has just found out about it and has fallen in a fit.'

Hilda stared. 'Who has?'

'Why, the orderly, of course!'

'But how could he have just –'

'Really, Van,' Lois interposed, and then, to Hilda,
'It's a joke, Hilda – and not a very nice one.'

Kit beamed. 'What would we do without you,
Willie, to keep us in our place?'

'Pla*ces*,' Lois said firmly, and was shushed by Sue.

'Go on, Hilda,' Connie said. 'Tell us!'

'Well,' Hilda said, pleased, 'they all went in there
last night – five of them – to have it out – I mean, it was
after the fifth one and she'd said the same thing –'

'*Hilda!*' Connie implored.

'Five what?' Sue asked. 'Have what out? You
sound like the dental clinic.'

'Pull yourself together,' Kit urged.

Hilda tried. 'It was the slips,' she said. 'And that
Meyers probationer – the one that looks like – like an
unbent hairpin. I mean, everybody, almost, who's
been in Miss Cameron's room lately, has come out
saying she said their slips showed, and they said she
said if they thought –' Hilda stopped and began again,
carefully, while Sue grinned across the table at Kit
and Connie.

'Five probationers,' Hilda said, coherent this time,
'and some regular nurses, and one *graduate*, all got
jumped on by Miss Cameron, you know.'

'I certainly do know,' said Sue. 'Go on. Where
were *you*? How did you hear about it?'

'Oh – er – well, I was over in Brewster, coming
along the corridor – and I saw all that mob – I mean,
the five probationers – kind of quaking outside Miss
Cameron's door – scared to death – and the Meyers
one was absolutely green – and that was funny, too,
because *she* was the one who said to come on – they
might as well die now as any other time – so they went

in. And – er – just then my shoe came untied – and I
stopped to fix it – so I couldn't very well help
hearing –'

'Naturally,' Lois said dryly, 'you had to tie your
shoe just there.'

Sue planted an elbow in Willie's ribs.

'Well, I *did* have to. I might have tripped on it.
Anyway, they went in – and Miss Cameron said in an
awful voice, "*What's all this?*"'

'And you,' said Lois, 'finished tying your shoe and
went right away, I suppose?'

'Do let her alone, Willie,' Connie said sharply. 'Go
on, Hilda!'

'So then nobody said anything for a minute, till
Meyers made kind of a funny noise. I know it was her
because Miss Cameron said what ailed her, Miss
Meyers, and don't stand there diddling and gobbling –
and Meyers gave sort of a squeak and said they'd
come about their slips –' Hilda stopped for a breath.

'Do get on, Hilda!' Kit said.

'Well, Meyers did all the talking – I didn't think she
had it in her – and she said there must be some
mistake about the slips because they didn't show –
and they'd come to Miss Cameron to ask her to help
them find out what the matter was – imagine that! –
and Miss Cameron said in an even awfuller voice,
"Your slip is showing *now*, Miss Meyers!" And would
you believe it, girls' – Hilda clasped her plump hands
and looked around the table, wide-eyed – 'would you
believe it – *Meyers* stood there right in Miss
Cameron's face and eyes and she said, "It *can't* be
showing, Miss Cameron, *because I took it off before I
came down here!*"' Hilda stopped again.

'Hurry *up*, Hilda,' Lois said involuntarily.

'Oo! Then the fur flew! Miss Cameron said did they mean to say they were going round the hospital without any underwear on and everything, and they said – I mean, Meyers said, well they had *some* on – and then everybody talked at once – and Meyers kept saying would Miss Cameron help them find out what the trouble was – and then, all of a sudden, Meyers said, "Oh, Miss Cameron – there it is! There it is!" And what do you think?'

'I'll bet,' Kit said, 'that it was Miss Cameron's slip dodging coyly around by itself!'

'Oh, no, it wasn't. I'm sure she had it on – or maybe she wears petticoats – but anyway, it seems Miss Cameron has some new bookshelves – right by the door – beside that screen, you know. And they have white silk curtains – and whenever the screen was up – and anybody came in the door, they stood in front of the bookcase to talk to Miss Cameron – and the bottom of the curtain showed below their skirt at the back!'

'Of course!' Sue cried. 'When Miss Cameron was sitting down she could just see the edge of the curtain, and it looked like something hanging off *us*! It was practically an optical illusion. *What* did Miss Cameron say?'

'Oh – at first she just said stand here and move there, and they all tramped around. Then, all of a sudden, she said "*Well!*" You know – with one of those awful snaps of hers – and everybody stopped talking as if they'd all been shot at once. And Miss Cameron's voice got all sort of funny, and she said, "I'm very sorry to have been so stupid and distressed you. I ask your pardon!" I must say, the old girl comes across when she comes across!'

'She's an old darling!' Sue said. 'What else?'

'Her voice got all kind of smiley, and she said she was glad they'd come to her, and it was very smart of Meyers to have seen what it was, and who thought of coming to her – and one of the probes said it was Meyers – and Miss Cameron was tickled to death and said it showed Meyers had character even if it *was* undeveloped. And she said, "I'm glad to see that I've been mistaken about you, Miss Meyers!" Can you beat it – Meyers doing all that!'

'You can't beat Miss Cameron,' Sue said. 'She'll be swell to Meyers from now on. What did Meyers say?'

'Why – I – didn't hear, because they started coming out just then – and – and I thought I'd better –'

'We get you,' Kit said. 'Don't bother to explain. And you'd better start eating, Hilda. It's ten to seven. Who's coming along?'

'We are,' said Connie and Sue together.

As they left the dining-room Connie murmured in Sue's ear, 'Well done, old thing!'

'Yes, wasn't it!' Sue returned. 'I've set Meyers up for life.'

'The think I like about you, Bat,' Kit said, 'is the way you always try to hide your light under a bushel.'

Sue grinned. 'My *lights*, you mean, don't you? Never mind, darling, when you're all grown up, maybe some day you'll have a nice, bright light of your own.'

Kit moaned feebly. 'Listen to her, Connie! She thinks she's puncturing me with her wit! Try a sledge-hammer, Sue dear. It would be much more subtle!'

'Go on!' Sue laughed. 'You're so full of holes now that anybody could tear you on the dotted line!' And with this final shot she turned quickly in at the door to Ward 8, leaving Kit speechless in the corridor.

8
Mr Tait

'What was the matter, Miss Barton?'

'I – don't know, Miss Lester. I just couldn't seem to do anything right. I'm terribly sorry.'

'I'm sorry, too, Miss Barton,' Miss Lester said gravely.

There were in one of the smaller operating rooms, where Sue, miserable and humiliated, was gathering up her instruments after an operation. Miss Lester had come in search of her after a brief conference with Dr Reed, the staff surgeon with whom Sue had been working.

'I put you in on that case,' Miss Lester went on, 'because you can be very quick when you choose. Dr Reed is impatient and he won't have a slow nurse, no matter how good she is otherwise. I'd hoped that you –' She hesitated, and then said quietly, 'I'm sorry to have to tell you this, Miss Barton – but I find your work disappointing. When you first came to the Amphitheatre I thought you were going to be one of my best nurses. Instead, your work has been progressively worse. You're almost through here – and if there isn't an immediate improvement I shall not be able to send in a good report of you. Can't you keep your mind on what you are doing?'

'I'll try,' Sue managed to say.

'I hope you will – because your next case is a gall

bladder with Dr Carson. I'll have to put you in on it because we have a heavy list to-day, and the other nurses will be tied up. Dr Carson is, if anything, worse than Dr Reed. I don't want a repetition of this last performance.'

'Yes, Miss Lester.'

Sue was left alone in the dishevelled operating room. The light from the big window seemed austere and threatening. The sheeted tables, the confusion of towels, the jumble of instruments, were silently accusing. She pulled off her rubber gloves and a hot tear fell on the back of her hand.

Miss Lester was right, of course. 'I can't seem to pay attention,' she thought. And as if things weren't bad enough she must start operating with Dr Carson, who scared everybody to death. Anyway, his operation was scheduled for eleven o'clock. It was only ten now. Sue would have time to pull herself together – if she could. But she did everything so badly these days! She'd been two months in the Amphitheatre, knew the work thoroughly, and got worse all the time. What was the matter? Why, even Kit, who had been operating only three weeks, was making a reputation for herself.

Sue carried her instruments to the sterilizing room, put the soiled sheets and towels in the laundry hamper, and went in search of Kit.

Kit was in the scrub room, lathered to the elbows. She looked over her shoulder as Sue came in.

'Finished already – good heavens! What's the matter? You look awful!'

'I've just had a bawling out from Lester. Dr Reed reported me.'

Kit's scrubbing-brush stopped abruptly in a snow of lather half-way up her arm.

'Why?' she asked.

'Oh, because I made a mess of things, as usual,' Sue said wearily.

'You have been sort of off your form lately. What happened?'

'I can tell you what happened, but I can't exactly tell you why. I gave him all the right things – at all the wrong times – and dropped the scissors on the floor – and didn't let go of a retractor when he said to – because I didn't hear him say it – and he cracked me over the knuckles with a pair of forceps – and finally he – he took my – table – away from me and threaded his own needles – and then I had to do the sponge count twice – and he swore!' Sue leaned against the wall and closed her eyes. Her lashes were wet.

'Gosh!' The sound of scrubbing resumed. 'I'm frightfully sorry, Bat. Haven't you any idea what's making you go off like that?'

Sue opened her eyes and stared through a blur at the white tiles of the opposite wall.

'Well,' she said slowly, 'Lester says I don't keep my mind on what I'm doing. I – suppose she's right.'

'Why don't you?'

Sue hesitated. 'I – I think,' she said miserably, 'that I'm – I'm bored.'

'*Bored!*'

'I know. It seems insane, when I've wanted operating so much.' She crossed to the sink and stood watching the rapid movements of Kit's brush. 'You see,' she went on, struggling to find an explanation, 'operating, for a nurse, isn't the way I thought it would be.'

'What on earth did you expect?'

'I guess – I thought we did a lot more – the kind of thing the house officers do – real assistance, you know.'

'But, Sue – we *do* give real assistance. You're crazy!'

'But it's so darned dull. Once you know what you're supposed to do – which isn't anything but hand up sponges and thread needles – you can't get any further. You might as well be water-boy on a baseball field.'

'Baseball isn't a matter of life and death. Operating is. Think what those men achieve every time they do an operation!'

'I have thought. I know the history of medicine just as well as you do. I appreciate what they're doing, and I think it's swell. But I can't help it if I'm not frantically interested in my part of it.'

'What do you want?'

'I don't know. I thought I wanted operating. But I don't want what this is. What's interesting about pushing catgut through the eye of a perfectly fantastic needle?'

'Nothing, I suppose, if you feel *that* way. I don't. I like the tables with the instruments all beautifully in rows. I like the feel of them. I like it when a surgeon sticks out his hand without a word – and shuts it on the instrument I put there – the *right* instrument. I like seeing that he has enough of everything. I feel as if I were practically making history every time I go in on an operation. It's exciting – and satisfying.'

Sue's eyes filled again.

'You're lucky,' she said with an effort. 'Oh, Kitty –

I *can't* be a flop at this – I simply can't! It'll bring down my whole record – and that's been pretty good so far.'

'I should say it has,' Kit said warmly. 'Don't worry, Bat. There's no good tying yourself in knots. Besides, I don't believe the Office will be as harrowed about you as you think. There must have been other perfectly good nurses who weren't so good at operating.'

'Maybe. But all the same, they expect you to be an all-round good nurse, and not one that just comes out in spots. Lester says if I'm not better she's going to send in a bad report of me – and on top of that she puts me in on a case with Dr Carson.'

'Carson!' Kit whistled. 'Oh, Bat! he's a holy terror. He eats nurses raw, for breakfast!'

'You're such a comfort!' Sue said faintly.

Kit was silent. She stepped on a pedal under the sink, letting the soapy water out of the bowl, stepped on another, and rinsed hands and arms under the clear stream that sprang from an overhanging faucet. 'I wish I could help you,' she said at last, 'but I don't know how. And I've got to go – right this minute. Let me know how you make out, will you? I'm – interested – you know that – don't you?'

'Yes, I know. And thanks a lot.'

Kit went away, leaving a trail of drops behind her, and Sue was alone again.

'There's no good hanging around here brooding.' she thought. 'I'd better go and do something.'

As she came out into the corridor the crisply white figure of Dr Barry emerged from a laboratory opposite. It would be a relief to tell him about her difficulties – but after all, it wouldn't be very tactful to tell a surgeon that you didn't like operating.

'Hello,' he said. 'I've been waiting for you to come out of there. I've a patient I wish you'd see for me.'

'I'd be glad to. Why didn't you come to the door?'

He grinned boyishly. 'That place is too exclusively feminine. You never know what you may find there. But seriously – there's an old man – Dr Carson's patient – waiting in the anæsthetic room. He's feeling pretty bleak. I wish you'd see if you can't brace him up a little – you have rather a way with patients.'

Sue's eyes lighted. This was something she *could* do.

'Of course! Thanks for telling me! – I'll see him now.' She hurried away.

Dr Barry stood motionless, one hand deep in a hip pocket, his eyes following Sue's red head and slender hurrying figure. Then his shoulders sagged. His face looked drawn and tired as he turned back to the laboratory.

Sue, in the anæsthetic room, was reading the patient's chart. Then she said:

'Good morning, Mr Tait.'

There was a slight movement from the stretcher.

'Good morning, nurse. Is – is it *time?*'

'Not quite,' very gently. She crossed to the stretcher. Her brown eyes, darkening with sympathy, took note of the frailty of the body under the white blanket; of the waxen pallor of the lined face; rested briefly on close-cropped grey moustache and white hair. The chart gave Mr Tait's age as sixty. He looked seventy.

The patient's eyes clung to Sue's face, avoiding the impersonal white room, the rows of ether cones, the gas-oxygen machine waiting in its corner. 'It – ain't time – yet?'

'I'm terribly sorry, Mr Tait, that you're having to wait like this. Is it getting on your nerves?'

'It does, kind of,' Mr Tait said. His grey moustache stirred in a half-smile, a pitiful attempt at non-chalance. 'Y'see,' he went on, 'I dunno how this is a goin' to turn out – not that it matters so much about that –' He stopped.

'What is it?' Sue encouraged.

'Well, what gets me down a mite is bein' so awful alone in this kind of a fix. A – a person needs somebody to kind of take an interest.'

'Haven't you any family?'

'I got a daughter – married – and out in California. But I – I didn't tell her about – this. I didn't want to worry her. I guess – maybe – if I'd realized how it was going to be – I might of weakened – though I dunno's I would at that – she sets considerable store by me.'

His daughter didn't know. And he wanted her – terribly. He wanted somebody with him who cared about him personally. What if it were her own father, Sue thought; her own father, alone – wanting *her* – afraid.

Her warm, strong young hand closed over Mr Tait's. She looked at him mistily.

'This is horrid for you,' she said, swallowing the lump in her throat. 'I'm *so* sorry. Will you believe me when I say that I would like – to take your daughter's place – while you're here – if you'll let me? I – I suppose it seems a funny thing for me to say – when I've just met you – but I care a lot how you feel – and what happens to you.'

Mr Tait's wise old eyes searched her face – questioning, relieved, touched.

'I – b'lieve you *do*, nurse,' he said at last. His moustache quivered, steadied. 'I dunno but what – if I hed another daughter – I'd like you to be her. It's mighty nice of you to be so kind to an old man.'

'I'm – not being kind. I feel that way. It happens that I'm going to help with your operation – so I can be with you all the time – even while you're asleep. And I think I can arrange it so I'll be with you on the ward when you wake up. All right? Would you like that?'

'I'd like it a heap. I feel better a'ready.' His faded blue eyes met hers in sudden appeal. 'Are ye – sure, nurse – that you'll be with me all the time?'

'I promise!'

The old man's eyes dimmed. 'Your father must be awful proud of you, nurse.'

'I hope he will be, some day,' Sue replied simply.

'What's your name?'

She told him.

'Miss Barton – Sue Barton,' he repeated after her. 'I guess I wun't forgit that name in a hurry.'

'And you won't feel alone any more?'

He shook his head.

Smiling, Sue lifted one finger in a brief salute. The smile was for Mr Tait – but the salute was for his daughter, far away in California. 'I'll have to go for a little while. You won't mind about the ether?'

'No, I wun't – not now.'

When Sue left the anæsthetic room she went at once to look over her table. It would be ready for her, of course, and anything she might do to it would only be as a gesture of keeping faith with Mr Tait – but it was a gesture she wanted to make.

She inspected the table carefully. When she was scrubbed she would add some extra needles, needle holders, and catgut. It would not be a bad idea, either, if she had another pair of gloves ready – not that they would be needed, but it would do no harm to have them – just in case.

While she was scrubbing she considered the situation. It *would* have to be Dr Carson, she thought miserably. She had never operated with him, but she knew that he was difficult and exacting. Miss Lester would be watching her every minute – and if Dr Carson had one of his fits of storming around, Miss Lester would think it was Sue's fault, whether it was or not. Sue's eyes filled with tears of nervousness which overflowed as another thought occurred to her. The other operating nurses were tied up now – but some of them would certainly be free before Sue's case was finished, and if Miss Lester didn't like the way things were going she would take Sue out of the operation and put another nurse in.

'And I *promised* I'd be with him all the time!'

She must keep that promise, no matter what happened.

Sue clung to this, resigning herself to the idea that her record was already ruined by the mere fact of her having to operate with Dr Carson. If only she could manage to stay through the operation. Perhaps if Dr Carson were in a good humour . . .

But Dr Carson was not in a good humour. Sue perceived that the moment his huge bulk and red face appeared in the operating room. He looked sharply at Mr Tait, now breathing quietly in the hands of the anæsthetist, and then, addressing the two operating nurses and his assistant house officers, Dr Sutton and Dr Parker, he remarked with ominous joviality that he supposed everybody was all thumbs – as usual.

The house officers exchanged uneasy glances. The anæsthetist looked at Sue, frankly sympathetic.

Miss Lester fastened Dr Carson's gown at the back and tied his mask. The big man, purring in his throat, snatched his gloves from the table without waiting for Sue to help him – a move which brought an unpleasant glare from Miss Lester, who seemed to be even more nervous than Sue herself.

Dr Carson strode across to the house officer's table. Still purring, he picked up an instrument, tried it, and with an unpleasant look at Dr Parker tossed it to one side. Sue's table was next.

'Where are my needle holders?'

'Right there, sir, under the towel.'

'What are *those*?'

'They – they're extra ones, sir, for emergencies. I thought if anything happened to your special ones –'

'You thought! I'll do the thinking here – and there won't be any emergencies!'

'Oh Lord!' breathed the other operating nurse in Sue's ear.

Dr Carson turned ponderously and his eye caught the quailing eye of the orderly.

'Who's that?'

Miss Lester explained hastily. They were shorthanded, and had had to put a new man in on Dr Carson's case. She was very sorry – but she was sure the orderly would be all right.

Dr Carson purred again and looked at his patient with a complete change of manner. For a brief moment the big man was anxious and kindly. The moment passed.

'Think you can keep this patient under long enough for me to do this operation?' he said to the anæsthetist.

She looked at him, outraged. 'Yes, sir.'

Dr Carson smiled unpleasantly behind his mask.

'Now if you boys can pull yourselves together –' He picked up the little knife.

There was a long silence. Sue, intent, thinking of little Mr Tait, whose life was in those big hands, kept the sponges coming, was ready with ties. Certainly Dr Carson, whatever his manner to his assistants, was one of the best surgeons Sue had ever known. She watched his hands, moving deftly, tenderly, with incredible speed and precision. And while he worked he missed no breath of the patient, no change in colour.

Dr Carson spoke suddenly. 'Get your little hands out of the way, Parker. Am I doing this, or are you?'

Dr Parker flushed. He hated being small – and Carson knew it.

There was another silence, broken only by Mr Tait's quiet breathing.

'Hot saline!' Dr Carson said sharply.

Sue hurried, soaking gauze in the hot fluid; handed it to Dr Carson; saw that he needed clamps – produced them. Dr Carson tested a clamp, which, with the perversity of inanimate things, suddenly refused to work. The big man uttered a single word and hurled the clamp across the room – almost in the face of an operating nurse who had appeared in the doorway.

'*Useless!*' Dr Carson shot at Sue, though whether he meant herself or the clamp she did not know, and, suddenly, didn't care. He was operating so beautifully on Mr Tait that it didn't matter what he said or threw.

Sue glanced at Miss Lester, who had taken a step towards the operating nurse in the doorway. Then she hesitated and looked back at Sue. Sue became a miracle of quickness, missing nothing, anticipating everything. Miss Lester relaxed.

Sue sent a thought toward the quiet figure on the operating table. 'I'm still with you, my poor dear.'

For a time everything went well. Once or twice when Sue had something ready before Dr Carson had time to ask for it, he gave her a curious, sidelong glance, and then unexpectedly, he turned and glared at her table.

Sue's heart turned completely over. She hadn't the least idea what he wanted.

'You think,' he purred at her, 'that you know everything. But you don't. *Orderly!*'

'Y-yes, sir!'

'Alcohol!'

The orderly, white-faced and bewildered, glanced at Sue, who nodded towards the rack on bottles along the wall. She couldn't possibly have anticipated this and Miss Lester must know it.

The orderly scuttled across the floor, his Adam's apple working like a piston, seized the bottle marked 'Alcohol,' – a huge five-pint bottle, and hurried forward.

Dr Carson thrust out his hand, holding a sponge, without looking up. Before anyone could move or speak, the flustered orderly, instead of pouring the

alcohol into a bowl, placed the heavy, unsterile bottle
in Dr Carson's outstretched palm, on the sterile glove
– which instantly ceased to be sterile.

There was a crash, and a roar.

The bottle splintered and the alcohol poured out
over the enraged surgeon's feet.

'You long-eared jackass!' he bellowed. *'Get out of
here!'*

The orderly fled, gibbering. Miss Lester cried out.
Dr Carson raged, his feet puddling in the alcohol, his
unsterile hand held away from him as though it were
leprous, while he tore off his gloves.

And then he turned on Sue. She heard the sharp
intake of his breath.

Quietly, before he could speak, she held out the
fresh pair of sterile gloves.

It was as though she had checked Niagara.

She saw the faces of the two house officers, mouths
open, waiting for the torrent of words. She saw Miss
Lester already quivering in anticipation. She saw Dr
Carson, purpling, speechless, his tantrum suspended.
They all looked incredibly silly, even the anæsthetist.

In spite of herself, Sue began to grin.

Dr Carson's eyes bored into hers.

'I've done it now,' Sue thought, sobering hastily.
'He knew I was laughing, in spite of the mask.'

She waited, her eyes on the rise and fall of Mr Tait's
chest – waited for the storm of anger that would send
her out of the operating room on the heels of the
orderly.

Dr Carson slid his hands into the gloves and went
back to work.

'Patient all right?' he said to the anæsthetist.

'Yes, sir. His pulse is a little weak, but he's doing nicely.'

There was no further conversation, but Sue, busy with needles, caught Dr Carson's eyes upon her. 'He's waiting,' she thought, 'to finish with Mr Tait before he blows me up.' And that was all right, because by then she would have kept her promise to the lonely little man – she would have been with him all the time; and that was all that mattered just now.

Dr Carson straightened up at last.

'All right, Parker. Finish it.' He took off his gloves and Miss Lester hurried to unfasten his gown. Freed of it, the big man stretched with a cracking of muscles. 'That nurse,' he said to Miss Lester – 'what's her name?'

It was coming now. Sue had made him ridiculous. She had dared to laugh at him. He wouldn't forgive her for that.

'Her name is Miss Barton, sir.'

'Barton, is it?' He glared at Sue; shifted the glare to Miss Lester, who wilted visibly. 'That's a young lady who thinks she's smart,' he said in his purring voice, with a jerk of his head toward Sue. 'And, by God, she *is* smart! Good operating nurse. Got a sense of humour.' He grinned suddenly. 'She laughed at me!' he said. '*Laughed!*' His roar of delight echoed in the white room. Then he addressed Sue. 'Don't lose your head when you work with me, do you? Why not?'

Sue's clear young eyes met his. She spoke with utter sincerity.

'You're such a marvellous surgeon, sir, that it doesn't seem to matter what else you do.'

'Well, I'll be –' He gave her a long look. Then,

unaccountably, he swallowed. 'Thank you,' he said gruffly. Then, 'Miss Lester, see that Miss Barton is always put in on my operations hereafter.'

'Certainly, sir!'

9
Connie has an Adventure

Sue was more depressed than cheered by her final success in the Amphitheatre, for she realized that it had been accomplished through her interest in Mr Tait; she still didn't like operating for its own sake.

'And that,' she thought, 'leaves me high and dry in the middle of my senior year – because I don't want to do operating when I graduate, and I'll have to be making up my mind what I do want.'

Perhaps Miss Waring could advise her. She always seemed to understand things.

Miss Waring did understand. Sue found her in her room, writing letters. The young head nurse looked up, her level grey eyes lighting with pleasure.

'Why, Sue Barton!' she exclaimed. 'Come right in. Here, let me get those things off the chair.'

'This is all right,' said Sue, dropping down on the bed. 'Please don't bother. I guess,' she went on, 'that you'll think I never come to see you unless I want something. I –'

'My dear, don't worry about that,' Miss Waring said cordially. 'I know what senior year is like. One never does any of the things one intends to do. Is anything the matter?'

'Well – yes. There is something.'

Sue explained her dilemma, and Miss Waring listened, nodding from time to time. 'You see,' Sue finished, 'I'd always thought I wanted to be an operating nurse. And it's sort of disconcerting to discover at the last minute that I don't like operating. I don't know what I do want – I mean, I don't know what I'm best suited for. I thought perhaps you could straighten me out.'

Miss Waring, leaning on her desk, chin in hand, looked at Sue thoughtfully.

'That's rather difficult,' she said at last. 'No one can really tell another person what to do. But I should say – at a guess – that your talent lies in your ability to deal with people. You go out to them. You like them, and they feel it. So naturally you wouldn't be particularly interested in operating. It's dramatic, but it's also coldly mechanical. You like the warmth of personalities.'

'That's exactly it!' Sue exclaimed, started.

'Then you want to choose a branch of nursing which will give you some scope for that. Perhaps you're an executive. Did you ever consider it?'

'No, I didn't.' Sue considered it now. 'But how am I going to know? Only a few of the girls get a chance to be staff nurses, and if I'm not one of the few how shall I find out whether I'm an executive or not?'

Miss Waring smiled. 'There you have me,' she said. 'I'm afraid there isn't anything to do but wait. Are you nearly through in the Amphitheatre?'

'Yes. I've had more than the twenty-five operations I need to take the State exams. I'll probably be out of the Amphitheatre any time now.'

'Then what?'

'Obstetrics, I suppose. Ten of my class are going to the James Memorial Hospital on the first of January. I'm pretty certain to be one of them.'

'Then perhaps you'll like maternity work. It –'

Sue shook her head. 'No. I think it will be frightfully interesting, but it doesn't appeal to me as a career.'

'Well –' Miss Waring abandoned obstetrics. 'Then that's out.'

Her suggestion about executive work remained in Sue's mind, however, and she discussed it with Kit and Connie that night.

'Maybe she's right,' Kit said, 'providing you can get the Office to let you be a head nurse. I'd like that myself. I never realized until I went to the Amphitheatre how much I liked organization.'

'What about you, Connie?' Sue asked idly.

Connie surprised them. She wanted to be an anæsthetist, she said.

'I'm crazy about it. I guess I must be an individualist. I like the way the anæsthetists sit, sort of withdrawn and unnoticed, and yet with everything depending on them. And every single case is different, no matter how many thousands you do. You have to have a kind of sixth sense. Anyway, I went to the Office to-day, and asked for the special course in anæsthetics. It –' She went on, bubbling with enthusiasm – little Connie, who had been so afraid of operations – until Kit remarked caustically to Sue:

'In case you want to know, Bat – Connie's going to be an anæsthetist!'

Connie laughed and subsided, and presently the talk turned to other matters – primarily the question of what they would wear to the house officers' dance, on Christmas Eve. Christmas was still three weeks away, but, as Kit said, it was never too early to think about clothes. And so, involved in this pleasant discussion, Sue forgot her problems for the moment.

She had been right, however, in thinking that she would go to the James Memorial Hospital with the January class. The Training School Office notified her of the fact within a week.

'But we are leaving you in the Amphitheatre until you go,' Miss Mason told her. 'Dr Carson has asked to have you stay on.'

This was pleasant to hear, at any rate, for as long as Sue had Dr Carson to manage she would do good work. She felt somewhat cheered, and settled down again in the Amphitheatre with the feeling that a month would be a long time if one spent it in worrying – so why worry?'

Meanwhile, winter set in with laden skies and the first soft feathers of snow. Sue, from an operating-room window, watched them floating aimlessly down, to cover the hospital grounds with a slowly deepening white.

The wards, she thought wistfully, would be a bustle of preparation for Christmas – and she wouldn't be there to help. A Christmas without patients would be pretty bleak – for now that she was senior nurse in the Amphitheatre she no longer went to Ward 8.

In the city streets the sounds of winter were beginning: the slurring of traffic; the beat of tire chains; the thin wail of whistles on hot-chestnut stands; the frosty tinkle of Salvation Army bells. At night the stars flared cold and green above the city, and shop windows glittered with Christmas decorations and coloured lights.

'Golly, but it's cold!' Connie said, bursting into

Sue's room late one afternoon. Her arms were filled with packages. Her eyes sparkled.

'You've been up to something,' Kit remarked lazily from the bed.

Sue was manicuring her nails by the window, settled deep in the only arm-chair. She looked up quickly at Kit's words.

'Come on, Connie,' Kit said. 'Out with it!'

Connie chuckled, spilled her packages impartially over Kit and the bed, and stood beaming.

'The most priceless thing has just happened to me,' she said.

'What?' from Kit.

'The nicest man I ever met in my life fell down the subway steps on me.'

'Fell –'

'Well, of course, if you *like* that sort of thing!'

'No, but honestly,' Connie bubbled, 'he was darling – not very tall, and blondish, and wears glasses. He – slipped on the steps just above me – and we both came down together – and all my bundles flew every which way – and he apologized like anything and gave me his card. Here!' She produced a calling card with the words 'Mr Philip Saunders' engraved on it.

'He's a poet!' Connie announced before the girls could speak.

Sue and Kit shrieked together.

'*A poet!*'

'*Whatever for!*'

'He's a good poet,' firmly. 'He's had three poems published. He showed me. He works on a newspaper – he's a copy writer, whatever that is – and –'

'I suppose he told you all this,' Kit remarked, 'while you were both sprawled on the subway floor. Did you bother to sit up, or did you just lie there and chat?'

'Don't be an idiot! He picked me up and chased my bundles and brushed me off and everything. He was terribly nice.'

'Well, when *did* he reveal ALL?'

Connie hesitated, flushing.

'Er – well,' she said, 'he – er – if you must know, he brought me home – er – after we'd had tea – and he told me all about himself on the way – I mean, what he didn't tell me while we were having tea.'

Kit chortled. 'Tea! He brought her home! Don't you know it isn't nice to talk to strange men you meet on the street?'

'I didn't meet him on the street. And it wasn't a pick-up, if that's what you mean. He gave me all kinds of references, and was so sweet – and asked so nicely if he might walk home with me.'

'So that makes it *not* a pick-up,' said the grinning Kit.

'Connie!' Sue cried. 'He gave you *references!* How Victorian of him – and how charming!'

'Yes, wasn't it?' said the unabashed Connie.

'So now,' Kit said, 'you have accepted his kind invitation to dinner, for to-morrow night.'

Connie's innocent hazel eyes rested on each of the girls in turn. 'As a matter of fact,' she said demurely, 'I've done just that. And what's more, I'm looking forward to it!'

With these startling words, she swooped up her packages and departed, leaving the girls staring at one another.

'Well, of all things!' Kit said slowly.

'I think it's lovely. He sounds nice.'

'Yes, he does. I hope something comes of it – if he *is* nice; she's had such a rotten time.'

'She certainly has.' She put down her manicure scissors and rose. 'How about some food, old thing? Want to go to first supper?'

'Yes, let's! I'm ravening! Shall we go and drag Connie from her dreams of the subway knight?'

'Uh-huh.' Sue stretched, and reached for her cap on the bureau. 'Come on.' As she moved toward the door she added as an afterthought, 'if it turns out to be all right, Connie ought to ask him to the house officers' dance.'

10
The Christmas Eve Dance

The most that the girls were able to discover about the mysterious Mr Saunders during the next three weeks was that he was quite as nice as Connie had expected. She continued to go out with him at least three times a week, and on the Sunday afternoons when she was off duty she disappeared without waiting for lunch, returning late in the evening with a new softness in her eyes and voice. She spoke of him occasionally as 'Phil,' but she said nothing about introducing him to Kit and Sue, who were devoured with curiosity.

'And I'm almost positive he's writing poetry to her,' Kit confided. 'I went up to her room last night to borrow some apron studs. Her door was open, so I walked in – and, my dear, she was reading something on a scrap of paper, and when I came in she turned as red as fire and sort of scrambled the paper into her pocket.'

'I'll bet that's what it was!'

'Why do you suppose she doesn't let us meet him?'

'Well,' said Sue after a moment's thought, 'I expect she just doesn't want anybody – even us – intruding, yet. She's so serious about the whole thing. But she's asked him to the dance! So we'll have to meet him.'

'How do you know she's asked him?'

'Because she said so, this noon, right out of a clear sky. We were going back the Amphitheatre from lunch, and were talking about the dance, and she said, sort of quietly and not at all like Connie – because she generally bubbles – "I've asked Phil to the dance, Sue – and he's coming – if he can borrow any evening clothes that will fit him – the poor sweet."'

'My gosh, Sue! Connie called him a "poor sweet"?'

'Yes, she did. And she announced that he was coming about the way you'd announce the President of the United States. But, Kit, he must be awfully poor if he has to borrow evening clothes. And Connie has so *much* money. Do you suppose he knows? He wouldn't be –' Sue paused, hating to suggest that Phil might be after Connie's money.

Kit shrugged and there the matter rested. As for meeting Phil, the girls' curiosity continued unsatisfied until the night of the dance.

The house officers always gave the Christmas Eve entertainment, and it varied in kind. The year before it had been a minstrel show, and Sue hadn't gone because she had had a bad cold. The year before that it had been a series of vaudeville sketches, the last and best of which had been written by Connie, to everyone's delight and amazement. The sketches had been followed by an impromptu dance.

This year there was to be only the dance, but it was to be a grand affair.

The house officers had borrowed the immense living room of Grafton House for the occasion – the living-room having ballroom proportions. They had hired caterers, and an eight-piece orchestra. Everybody was invited and could bring friends. For three days before Christmas, nurses, wandering casually about Grafton Hall in pyjamas or dressing-gowns, had retreated hastily at the sight of boyish figures in white clambering up ladders in the living-room. Night nurses complained of hammering. The Hall maid stepped on a large tack, and had to be taken to the Emergency Ward to have it removed. But by Christmas Eve the nurses had become accustomed to beholding their living-room transformed into a forest of green boughs, to pricking themselves on holly, and to speculating on the results of hanging mistletoe over every door.

It was fun dressing for the dance. Sue had been so long in uniform that white satin underwear and chiffon stockings made her feel like an entirely different person. It was hard to believe that the feet on which she was strapping frivolous silver sandals could be the same feet which had stood all day on the tiled floor of the Amphitheatre.

'Sue!' Kit said outside the door. 'Are you dressed? Can I come in?'

'Of course!'

The door opened and Kit rustled in, her black tulle skirt swirling around the slender arrow of her body.

'*Kitty!*' Sue cried. 'How marvellous! That dress makes you look like a movie about international spies!'

'Does it?' Kit beamed. 'I hoped it would. Black always makes me feel as if I had a frightfully interesting past, full of duels and suicides, and all that. Do hurry, Sue! *Phil's* here! And Connie has gone down.'

'*Honest?* So we meet him at last! How does she look?'

'Just as you'd expect – in turquoise – simply darling!'

But it's more than that – she looks as if something were lit inside her. Do you think love would do that for me?' Kit surveyed herself in the mirror with intense interest.

Sue laughed, and, picking up the mist of smoke-blue chiffon that lay across a chair, slipped it over her head. The soft folds whispered down over silken underwear and settled about her gratifyingly.

'Golly!' Kit said, frankly staring. 'You – I don't mean to seem so surprised, but that dress really does things for you.'

Pleased, Sue's glance went to the mirror, to rest on the reflection of smoky blue that brought out the brightness of her hair and the transparency of her skin. Her eyes shone, wide and dark.

'It *is* nice, isn't it?' Sue agreed, and then laughed in sheer excitement. 'I feel glamorous myself, if anybody should ask you.'

She put a final dab of powder on her nose and slipped into the black velvet evening wrap that her mother had made for the dress.

'Come on,' she said briskly. 'I'm *dying* to get a look at Phil!'

The elevator, complaining bitterly as usual, deposited them on the first floor, and they saw Phil and Connie sitting decorously in one of the little alcoves off the living-room.

Connie came to meet them, tiny and delicate, in a sheen of turquoise, with that softness in her eyes.

'You look lovely!' she exclaimed; then, eyes suddenly shy, 'Come and meet Phil.'

He stood waiting in the alcove, a short, earnest young figure in black and white, and at Connie's nod he came forward hastily. Sue looked at him and liked what she saw – liked his firm chin and grave mouth. His grey eyes, behind shell-rimmed glasses, were steady, gentle, and warm with friendliness as they looked into her own.

Sue breathed a sigh of relief. This was no fortune-hunter. This was a very nice boy.

'I've been explaining to Connie,' he said shyly, 'that if she heard a noise like a pistol-shot she isn't to pay any attention. This stiff shirt belongs to somebody a good deal bigger than I – and it keeps making noises like an iceberg cracking up.' He grinned. 'Any minute,' he added, 'it may pop open – the way they do in the comedy shorts.'

'He's a darling,' Sue thought, and smiled at him.

'If it does,' she said, 'just tie a wreath of holly to your collar, and we'll tell people you're eccentric –' She broke off as Bill's voice said:

'Merry Christmas!'

Sue turned. 'Why, *Bill*!' she exclaimed. 'Forgive me if I seem a little faint. You look so – so awfully impressive. I've – never seen you in dinner clothes –'

Barry flushed, smiling at her above gleaming shirt front and black tie. '*You're* – lovely,' he said.

Sue remembered her manners. 'Bill, this is Mr Saunders – Dr Barry.'

The two men clasped hands warmly, and Sue thought, 'Bill likes Phil Saunders – so he *must* be all right.'

The room was beginning to be crowded, and the orchestra, which had been making discordant sounds, suddenly melted into a soft, crooning beat.

'Shall we dance?' Bill asked.

He danced moderately well, threading his way with a worried frown among the shifting couples on the floor. There were not many uniforms present – a few, here and there – but for the most part nurses and doctors were almost unrecognizable in evening clothes.

Bill made desultory conversation. Like most unsure dancers, he seemed to feel that talking covered a multitude of sins. Sue murmured replies. It was pleasant, dancing with Bill. His shoulder, in the smoothly fitted black coat, was close to her cheek. It looked very broad and safe and steady – a good shoulder to lean upon, if necessary.

A hand caught Sue's elbow and the handsome, complacent face of George Lamson loomed before her. Bill turned away without a word.

Sue had never danced with anyone like Dr Lamson. He led effortlessly, skilfully, melting into the throb of the music, holding her close – too close. Sue drew away slightly, but he clasped her again. He made no remark until the dance finished and he returned her to the little alcove. Then he said, 'May I have the next?'

Philip Saunders heard him and caught Sue's glance of appeal.

'Sorry,' he said quickly, 'but I think the next is ours – isn't it, Sue?' His tone implied previous agreement and a long acquaintance.

'That was nice of you,' Sue said, when they moved out on the floor. 'It isn't that I dislike Dr Lamson. It's just that he's a little too prevalent at times.'

'Let me know any time you want to get rid of him,' Phil said quite grimly, and Sue wondered if all men disliked Lamson at sight. She looked over Phil's shoulder for Bill, but he was nowhere around. He'd been very cross when he went away. Well, he'd have to get over it.

The orchestra was excellent and the excitement of Christmas was in the air. Young feet, tired with tramping the hard hospital floors, lost their tiredness and moved swiftly and smoothly to the rhythm of the music. Now and again the maid came to the door with a whispered word for some young doctor, who departed hastily. Night nurses, in uniform and ready for duty, paused in the doorways and were seized by exuberant house officers with pleas for 'just one dance.' Eyes sparkled. There was laughter, chatter, singing.

Sue danced with Dr Parker, who had waited eagerly for the chance, and was openly and bitterly disappointed when Dr Lamson cut in. She danced again with Bill, who had returned smiling and quite composed – and she felt suddenly and abruptly happy. It was a gorgeous evening – gorgeous music. And it was Christmas Eve.

Phil Saunders, when he could bear to leave Connie for a brief interval, was pleasantly attentive. Once, when Sue was dancing with him, he said to her wistfully, 'Would – would you tell me about Connie – I mean, what she's like to be with all the time? She seems so lovely and remote to me. I'd like to know what she's like to her friends.'

'She's one of the dearest persons I ever knew,' Sue replied warmly. 'And besides that she's the best sport in the world. You should have seen her pushing me up the ivy vines of the nurses' home the night we got locked out, and she and Kit waited hours in the cold for me to let them in.' She told him the details of that escapade.

He roared with laughter.

'I knew she was wonderful!' he said.

Dr Lamson made his inevitable appearance when the next dance began, and swept Sue away before Phil could recover from his absorbed thoughts of Connie. Lamson was behaving better now, but Sue was grateful for the eagle eye of Miss Mason, which rested upon him coldly.

At ten minutes to eleven the night nurses departed reluctantly to their wards, leaving behind the music and the fun.

'Which is too bad,' the ever-present Lamson said in Sue's ear, 'because there will be more men to cut in on me now, and I'd like you to myself.'

'Don't be silly,' Sue returned crossly.

He ignored this. 'You might not believe it,' he said, guiding her expertly out of the way of big Dr Earle and his partner just in time to avoid a collision, 'but I've been thinking up a very graceful little speech to make to you – only now I find I can't make it. I can only say – how lovely you are.'

'I wish you wouldn't go on like this. It isn't at all necessary.'

'Not nec –' he began, laughing. Then he sobered. 'My dear,' he said serenely, 'you'll just have to get used to my telling you that you're lovely – because you are, you know, and I expect to tell you so very often.' His eyes searched her face, sure of their power.

Sue moaned inwardly.

'I'm sorry to be rude, Dr Lamson,' she said,

slipping out of his arms, 'but I'm rather tired. If you'll excuse me –' She caught up her skirt with one hand and was gone through the crowd in a flutter of chiffon.

Sue went up to her room, applied a little fresh lipstick, and came down again. The music had stopped. She paused in the doorway and saw Bill across the room, talking with one of the house officers, his white shirt front gleaming against the dark background of branches. Sue smiled, compelling him with her eyes. After a moment he looked up, and his glance flickered uncertainly around the crowded, noisy room. In another second he would see her and come. Sue's smile was very confident.

His eyes strayed nearer, and then – a tall, striking-looking girl with predatory eyes intercepted his look with a flutter of her hand. Bill bowed to her politely, excused himself to the house officer, and crossed the room, tall, aristocratic, unconcerned.

The dark-eyed nurse gave him a slow upward glance as he joined her.

Sue's smile faded. She'd been waiting for him, expecting him. And he had been looking for her – she knew it. But when Eleanor Gerard waved, he went to *her*.

Sue stepped back from the doorway, considering a moment, and then went down the stairs to the basement.

Refreshments were to be served on a long table in the little basement living-room, off the kitchenette, and the caterer's men were already busy there. Sue wandered along the corridor in a rustling of silk and approached the table. It looked very pretty, she thought. The caterer's men had arranged it with

professional showmanship, and the plates of sandwiches, cake, tiny sausages, cold meats, and salted
nuts were more than appetizing – if one were hungry.
There was even chicken in aspic. Those poor boys
must have spent every penny they had on this outlay.

'Help yourself, miss,' said one of the men.

Sue picked up a salted nut, bit into it reflectively,
tried a tiny sandwich, and finally sat down on the arm
of a chair to stare absently at the silver toe of her
sandal.

Had Bill seen her smiling at him, or hadn't he?'
Even if he hadn't, why did he want to rush over to
Eleanor Gerard? There'd been something very
intimate in the way she looked up at him – as though it
hadn't been the first time. Of course, she was a very
pretty girl. Still . . . Sue was startled at her feeling of
possessiveness about Bill. Was she being that loathsome thing – a dog in the manger? How rotten of her!
She rose abruptly and moved to the window, her
lower lip caught between her teeth, and paused
motionless, unseeing eyes fixed on the windowpane,
which reflected the warmly lighted room, the flicker
of the open fire, the gay table.

Bill found her there at last.

'Where've you been?' he asked. 'I've been looking
for you everywhere.'

'Have you?' She looked up at him 'I *was* waiting for
you.'

'Here?' He was astonished.

'No – upstairs. But after a while I got tired of
waiting and came down here.'

'Why didn't you let me know? You could have
given me a high sign, or something. I didn't see you.'

'I *know* you didn't.' It was her own voice speaking, saying stupid things, but she couldn't seem to stop it. It went on without her volition. 'You seemed to be having a good time with Eleanor Gerard – and I'm afraid I'm not very aggressive.'

'What's the matter, Sue?' he asked, really concerned. 'You aren't like yourself at all.'

The caterer's men were watching them.

'It's nothing, Bill,' Sue said wearily. 'I'm a little tired, I think.'

'Look here,' he said eagerly, 'how about a little fresh air? Shall I get your wrap?'

'If you like. It's upstairs in the alcove.'

He returned with the wrap in a few moments, helped her on with it, and they went through the underground passage that led to the interior grounds of the hospital. It was strange to be wandering around with Bill like this, undisturbed by the thought of meeting a supervisor. It would be stranger still to be away from it all.

'I'm going to James Memorial the first of January,' she said suddenly.

'But that's next week!' he was startled. 'And I – I won't see you for three months!'

'Oh,' lightly, 'I shall be around from time to time – on my afternoons off. It's not Siberia, you know. It's only in the suburbs.'

He was silent, opening the door to let her pass, and they stepped out into a white world of moonlight and snow. It was a clear still night. The air was like splinters of glass against their faces. Sue gathered up her skirt and they moved on, down a little walk, under bare elm branches black against the sky. The snow squeaked under their feet and their breaths mingled in a white cloud before them.

Sue slipped her free hand through Bill's arm, feeling the hardness of muscle under his black coat sleeve.

'I'm sorry I was so irritable, Bill,' she said at last. Then, as he was silent, 'Is – is there anything I can do – to make up for it?'

'You – don't have to do anything,' he said in a low voice. 'You've already done it – long since.'

'What on earth do you mean?'

Bill stopped in the path and turned to face her. Her hand dropped from his arm. She looked up at him, wondering. Around them the hospital lights – the lights of the world – twinkled across the expanse of snow. He took a deep breath.

'Will you marry me, Sue?'

Sue's throat closed. She stared at him, white and stunned – speechless. And without warning there came a clamour of sound – chimes, sweet, clear, imperative – swinging out across miles of moonlit winter air. Christmas morning! And he was waiting for his answer.

'I had to tell you,' he said. 'I love you – so much.'

The silver voices of the chimes beat above his head – his dear, dark head, outlined in moonlight, bent a little, waiting.

Sue drew a quivering breath and put her hand on his arm. Her voice was very gentle.

'Bill dear,' she said, 'will you understand when I say that I love you very much – but I don't know whether I'm *in* love with you or not? Because, you see, I'm rather frightened of marriage. I – I don't feel ready for it – and I would, wouldn't I, if I were in love?'

'I don't know,' he said. 'I think so.'

'I've been just myself so long' – she was pleading with him now – 'and when you're married you're part of someone else. I don't know – whether I'd like – to stop being myself. I mean – I don't know what marriage ought to be. Or – or if it's worth it. I only know that you're the best friend I have – or could want to have.'

He was silent.

Sue's fingers trembled on his sleeve. 'It – it means an awful lot to me – your friendship. Is it – very hard for you – to be just friends? Could you try – *would* you keep things as they have been?'

'Yes,' he said.

'Th-thank you.' She hesitated. Then, timidly, 'Have I spoiled everything?'

'No, dear.' His hand was warm, reassuring, closing over her cold fingers. At last he said, 'You're getting your feet wet. Shall we go in?' He smiled at her in the moonlight.

They turned back along the snowy path, moving in the crystal music of chimes. There was a dull pain in Sue's chest. She'd hurt him – awfully. As they reached the shadow of the doorway she looked up at him, her eyes clear and tender in the starlight.

'Perhaps,' she said, 'if I had a little time – if you could bear to be patient, Bill – I – I would *like* to be in love with you –'

Before he could speak she lifted slim hands to draw his head down, and kissed him – a child's kiss, wistful and apologetic.

The door burst open in a rush of warm air and a babble of voices and laughter. Half a dozen young nurses, gay in silks and chiffon, and followed by a phalanx of black coats and white shirt fronts, streamed out into the cold.

'Merry Christmas, Bat! Merry Christmas, Dr Barry!'

They had seen nothing.

Little Dr Parker pounced on Sue. 'Here's the red-headed wench! This is going to be my dance – aw, please!' He caught her hand and pulled her, laughing, into the passage-way. She looked over her shoulder at Bill before she went – a look so sweet that hot colour flooded his face and he turned back into the concealing dimness of the moonlight.

The nurses and their escorts trailed down the path, leaving him standing there. Voices and laughter came back to him through the brittle cold, but he did not hear. He was standing motionless, staring at moonlit snow with eyes that saw nothing – for they were blind with hope.

11
A New Side of Life

The James Memorial Hospital took only maternity cases. It was a small, semi-private hospital located just outside the city limits, and its reputation was such that even great training schools sent their students to it for the three months' course in obstetrics.

Ten seniors left for James Memorial on the first of January. Connie, to Sue's delight, was among them. She would not begin anæsthetics until her return. The only other one of their immediate friends in the group was Francesca Manson – if her not too amiable detachment could be called friendship.

Connie was unconcerned about leaving. James Memorial was only an hour by bus from the city and Phil could visit her there almost as easily as in town.

'Besides,' Connie said happily to Sue on the way out, 'it's in the country. Phil adores the country and so do I. Even if it is winter there's so much we can do – skating, tobogganing, long walks!'

Sue listened, feeling rather left out. Everything was 'Phil' nowadays and there was no Kitty to turn to, for Kit was still in the Amphitheatre, and could only pay the girls flying visits. It wasn't so much fun being a senior. The first two years the girls had been together all the time. Now they were continually being separated. Even Bill was out of the picture for a while, for he, of course, could not visit Sue. She would miss their pleasant talks and the new feeling of understanding between them, though her three months' absence would have its advantages, for she would have time to think things out – to get another perspective, if possible. But she felt lonely nonetheless.

The girls found the James Memorial a startling contrast to their own school. They were accustomed to acres of buildings; to enormous wards; to a staff numbered by the thousands; to nurses' homes as large as hotels. The James Memorial consisted of a single three-storey building, with a wing in which the nurses lived. The largest ward contained twelve beds. There were three tiny operating rooms – called 'case rooms,' here. Corridors were scarcely more than a hundred and fifty or two hundred feet long, and in the nurses' wing there were exactly two bathrooms for the students. The staff consisted of a superintendent of nurses, her assistant, a night supervisor, three staff nurses, and some thirty nurses, all from outside schools.

But it was a pretty little hospital, with spacious grounds and sun-rooms on every floor, and the wards and private rooms were charmingly decorated.

'Goodness! It's like living in a chintz thimble!' She said to Connie as they surveyed their room. That was another thing – two girls to a room. Sue had never lived so intimately with anyone before, and was not at all sure how she would like it – even with Connie.

They had supper that night in a tiny dining-room which had only six tables.

'I feel like Alice in the Rabbit's house,' Connie murmured in Sue's ear as they sat down.

'Me, too! Oh, Connie – what a marvellous school ours is! I'd never realized –'

There were a number of nurses from their own school who had been two months or more at James Memorial, and after supper there was a general reunion in the living-room of the nurses' wing, where Sue, asking questions, learned that they would have two weeks' duty in the wards, taking care of mothers; then a month of case room, a month of nursery, and two weeks' night duty. There was an exchange of gossip and news, and then the conversation turned to babies. The new girls were yet to learn that in James Memorial all conversation turned to the subject sooner or later.

The nurses smiled, speaking of babies. Their faces softened. Their voices took on a new quality – of tender amusement. They spoke endlessly of babies.

Sue was surprised and a little startled by this – the nurses seemed so unusually absorbed. Sue knew very little about babies, especially tiny ones – except that she had heard they were red-faced and could not see. She had given hardly any thought to them. They were a part of maternity work, which was a part of her training – and that was all.

So in spite of the evening's conversation she was totally unprepared for what took place at nine o'clock next morning.

The class were given careful instructions on the care of new mothers, and then were sent to various parts of the little hospital for duty. Sue was sent to the twelve-bed ward.

It was like any ward, except for being small. The patients were like any patients. They talked, slept, read, knitted, wanted this or that. Baths were given. Beds were made.

Sue paid very little attention to the time, beyond thinking that here it was, only nine o'clock, and she was already nearly through her work – had, in fact, reached the final stage of changing water in the vases of flowers. She was setting a vase of roses on a bedside table when she became aware of a change in the ward.

Patients who were reading stopped suddenly. Knitting was laid aside. Sleeping patients woke with a start. Even the other nurses paused in their work.

There was a ripple of movement around the ward; an excited stirring.

'What is it?' Sue asked a patient.

The woman's eyes misted. 'Listen!' she said.

Sue listened – and from a distance came the sound of an elevator door opening. With that sound was another, increasing in volume, lusty, continuous, unmistakable – the indignant squalling of hungry babies. Sue was caught up in the tide of emotion around her – was bewildered by it.

A moment later the long whiteness of a truck came to a stop before the door. Padded sideboards concealed its frantic occupants. Sue went to the door and looked into the truck.

Twelve babies lay on their sides in a row, squirming, flourishing, kicking, yelling – and gobbling at the backs of each other's head.

'*Oh!*' said Sue faintly.

The nurse in charge of the truck scooped up two babies, glancing at silver tags hanging on chains around fat necks, and went into the ward, a baby under each arm. She returned empty-handed, and scooped up two more. Within three minutes there was not a sound in the ward.

Sue stood in the doorway, watching the mothers.

In all twelve beds there was peace and quiet. The mothers lay motionless, their eyes on the tiny heads close beside them. Dark Italian faces, nervous Jewish faces, high-cheekboned Irish and Scandinavian faces – all held the same tremulousness of wonder and delight.

Sue's throat tightened.

'Goodness!' she thought. 'I'd no idea it was like this!'

She waited, fascinated, until the babies' nurse returned. Then she stepped into the corridor to ask if she might help take the babies out.

'Surely. Here – I'll show you.' The nurse brought out a baby with appalling casualness. 'Like this,' she said, holding the baby under her arm as if it were a bag of laundry. 'Its body rests between your hip and your arm. You support its spine with your arm, and its head with the palm of your hand. You want to be very careful about their heads – always slip your hand under the head before you pick up a baby.'

'But – it seems so impolite to hold it that way.'

The nurse laughed.

'Not at all. It's the only way to carry a very little baby – under your arm. Its head and spine are supported. You can't drop it. It can't roll out from between your hip and your arm, and it remains in a horizontal position. I assure you,' she added, 'it's a mistake to hold a baby upright when its stomach is full.'

They went into the ward and Sue picked up a

sleeping baby, imitating the other nurse as exactly as she could. It was quite simple. The little bundle fitted snugly under her arm. It was also a very damp bundle – but no matter. Sue felt the round head, warm and fuzzy, in her hand, and her heart contracted. She had never known so strange or so profound a feeling.

The baby's tiny hands were relaxed; its eyes were closed; its fraction of a month was open – and to Sue's utter delight it gave a faint but definite snore.

Sue blinked rapidly as she carried the baby away – followed by the yearning eyes of its mother.

By ones and twos, limp and replete, the babies were taken out, and the truck went silently back along the corridor to the elevator.

When it had gone there was a buzz of happy conversation around the ward, and then, gradually, knitting was resumed and books were opened.

Sue returned to her work rather shaken.

Four times a day the babies came down. Sue quickly became accustomed to handling them, but their appeal grew rather than lessened. At first they all looked alike to her, but in a few days she perceived that they were as different as grown people, and the nursery nurse told her that they had distinct personalities. Sue found this difficult to believe – of such tiny babies.

'All right,' the nurse told her, 'wait until you have nursery duty, and you'll see.'

Sue was looking forward to this, now, with growing impatience, but she knew that she must have a month of case room first and tried to resign herself to the wait. Meanwhile she was growing used to having a room-mate and found it pleasant. Connie was such a dear – always quiet, considerate, and companionable. They lay awake too long at night, talking, but it was worth it. Sue was getting to know Connie better than she had ever known her. They talked about almost everything – life and love and babies and the future and Phil. Only one topic was never mentioned – Bill. Sue didn't know why she was so reticent about him.

He was writing to her quite regularly – gay, amusing, friendly letters, full of news of the hospital. He made no further reference to being in love with her, and Sue was both relieved and disappointed.

Her two weeks on the ward seemed like a minute. She was in her element now that she had patients again. Everything pertaining to them interested her – their comfort, their histories, and most of all their point of view about having babies.

There was the mother of five – now the mother of six – a big, fair-haired woman, with broad, freckled face, who hoped that she would have at least five more babies.

'I *couldn't* have too many,' she said. 'Every one is welcome.' Her other children came to see her and the new baby. They were beautiful children, grey-eyed and fair like their mother. They had happy faces.

There was the eighteen-year-old bride who looked at her baby with loving but astonished eyes. She was glad to have him, though one, she thought, was enough.

'Don't ye belave it, dearie,' said an enormous Irish scrubwoman from her bed in the corner. 'This is me siventeenth – tin of thim livin'. I comes here iviry year, reg'lar as th' clock – an' think nothin' of it!'

There was the thin, bitter woman in the bed by the

door. Her husband didn't like children and never once came to see her. She clung to her baby as though it were the only thing left to her – as it undoubtedly was.

At the end of two weeks. Sue was transferred to the second-floor private rooms, from which she was to be on call for the case room, and it was here that she had an amusing experience.

One of her patients was a stoutish, amiable, middle-aged woman who had been married fifteen years and had given up hoping for the baby that never came. When it did come she was dazed and happy, but incredulous. Her son was three days old when she became Sue's patient, and she had not yet seen him, for she had been quite ill.

'Are you *sure* I've got a baby?' she asked Sue.

'I'm not only sure – I'm going to bring him to you right now. To-day is the day for his first feeding.'

Mrs Millson sat up, round-eyed and excited. 'Can I *really* see him now? Oh, do *hurry*, Nurse Barton!'

'I will – but you lie right down, at once!'

'Oh yes, yes indeed – anything you say. Will – will it do the baby any harm if I sit up?'

'Why, no, of course not. But it isn't good for *you*. What's the matter?'

'I – I'm scared. I – don't know anything about babies. What'll I do with it?'

'Don't worry. I'll show you.'

Sue went out to the nursery.

'May I take Baby Millson?' she asked the nurse, who was just leaving, with a baby under each arm.

'Sure. Go ahead!'

Sue picked up the hearty eight-pound baby, who

puffed and waved his fists, but didn't cry. She carried him down the corridor.

Mrs Millson's eyes were enormous when Sue came in the door. She raised herself on an elbow and peered, breathless, at the tiny red face.

'Oh!' she wailed. 'Is – is he deformed?'

'Certainly *not*!' Sue was outraged.

'B-but he – he's so funny-looking!'

'All new babies look like that. He's a *beautiful* baby.'

'I-is he?' – relieved.

Sue laid the baby on his mother's arm and settled him for a substantial meal.

Mrs Millson looked up at her with tearful eyes.

'I – I don't care if he – he *is* ugly – so there! He's *my son*!'

Sue swallowed. 'He's one of the finest babies in the nursery.'

Mrs Millson touched the down on her son's head. 'Can I move at all – while he's here?'

'Surely – he won't break, you know. He's a very husky young man. I have to go now – but ring if you want anything.'

Sue retired to the kitchen to make cocoa, and for a few minutes the ward was silent.

Then a bell whirred – and kept on whirring with alarmingly urgency, accompanied by screams. Mrs Millson's voice shrieked, '*Help! Help! Nurse Barton!*'

Sue rushed from the kitchen and down the corridor to Mrs Millson's door.

Mrs Millson was safe in bed – her thumb on the bell. The baby lay on her arm.

'*Nurse Barton! Nurse Barton! Quick! The baby's dying!*'

Sue rushed to the bed, her heart pounding, and looked at the baby. Mrs Millson was greenish-white with terror.

Sue straightened up with a gasp of relief.

'He's perfectly all right, Mrs Millson – and sound asleep. Wha – what happened?'

'*Asleep!*' Mrs Millson collapsed on her pillow. 'Oh, my, Nurse Barton! I was so frightened. He – he was eating – and all of a sudden the milk all came up – and he didn't eat any more – and I – I thought – oh dear!'

Sue leaned weakly against the wall.

'Don't *ever* scare me like that again,' she said. Then she laughed. 'He ate too fast, Mrs Millson, that was all. He regurgitated. It's nothing. All babies do it. I didn't think to tell you that you mustn't let him gobble. *Bad boy!*' She picked up the placid baby. '*Greedy!*'

Mrs Millson beamed at the portly infant. 'Isn't he *wonderful*!' she said. 'And so smart! Imagine him doing that! But – I – I guess you'd better take him now. I – don't seem to be able to manage him. I guess he's going to be a handful. He's smarter than his mother.' She smiled proudly. 'Just wait till my husband hears what his boy did!'

12
Case Room

It was a little like operating – technically. There was the same routine of keeping things sterile, and the familiar scrub. But there the similarity ended, for, except for an hour or so, work in the case room consisted of waiting; of talking with the patients and encouraging them; of checking up on innumerable details. Then, after tedious hours which terminated at last in a flurry of excitement, there would be the baby.

Always, Sue thrilled to that first cry of the newborn child.

Sometimes the baby didn't cry, and that nearly always meant that he hadn't begun to breathe. So his welcome into the world was a brisk spanking administered by the doctor. If there was still no gasp, followed by a yell of protest, the baby was plunged first into cold water, and then into hot water.

Sue was appalled by such harsh treatment, and gentle little Connie's eyes filled with horrified tears the first time she witnessed this performance. It did not often occur, however, and the girls, though shocked, knew that it was necessary.

Before Sue's training-school days she had heard tragic stories of babies being mixed in hospitals, and she discovered that some of the patients, especially those who were having their first hospital experience, still believed that it could, and might, happen. Sue got a great deal of satisfaction from proving to them that no such thing was possible. The very instant the baby was born, she assured them, a silver chain, with a tag bearing the baby's name, the name of its mother, her ward, and the number of her bed, would be fastened about the baby's neck. The baby would still be wearing chain and tag when it left the hospital – so no mistakes *could* be made.

Case-room duty offered interesting sidelights on human-nature, and presented some odd problems.

What to do with the husbands was one of these. All husbands, it seemed, were equally difficult – and one felt so sorry for them. They sat waiting, or paced the floor, in the hospital waiting-room, while their sons or their daughters were being born. They bit at their fingernails. They picked their ties apart. They pulled all the buttons off their vests and coats. They twisted their hats out of shape. They swore and they perspired. Sometimes they fainted. Always they rushed after every passing nurse, to hold her by the apron and plead in a hoarse voice for the latest bulletins from the case room.

There was nothing that one could do for them. They were too upset to read anything or carry on a conversation. They could only walk the floor or sit huddled by the door, with wilting collars and dishevelled hair. Their wives in the case room worried about them. 'Is John still here? Tell him to go home. Tell him I'm fine.'

The nurses carried them coffee, soothed them, revived the faint with brandy, urged them to go home. But they refused to leave. Even those husbands who, for one reason or another, were unable to be present seemed to spend all their time at the telephone.

Once Sue had occasion to take a long-distance call from a Mr Jackson, whose wife had come to the hospital the day before and had gone to the case room that morning.

'How is Mrs Jackson?' he asked in the customary desperate voice. 'Has the – the baby come?'

'Mrs Jackson is doing splendidly,' said Sue, grinning. 'And you have two fine little girls.'

'What?'

Sue repeated her statement.

The voice at the other end of the wire became impatient. 'No! No! I said Mrs *Jackson! Mrs Willis Jackson!* I want to know how she is!'

'Mrs Willis Jackson is doing nicely. She has two little girls.'

'Two what?'

'Girls – two girls – *twins!*'

'Twi – *good God!*' There was silence.

After a while Sue hung up.

In the case room itself, however, Sue found that no mother behaved alike. And two of them she was to remember all her life.

Her third day on duty there, she was told to stay with a young woman who was having her first baby. First babies are usually slow in arriving, and Sue and her patient had a great deal of time for conversation.

Sue had never seen any woman who wanted a baby quite as frantically as this one. She was about twenty-five – slender and dark-haired, with a pale, transparent skin. When she spoke of the baby her eyes shone a deep blue, and her lips quivered.

'All my life I've longed for a baby,' she said. 'Now it's coming I can hardly believe it – it doesn't seem as if I deserve so much happiness.'

'Have you been married very long?'

'Two years.'

'I suppose your husband is pleased, too?'

'Tom?' Her eyes filled with happy tears. 'He – he almost cried when I told him – and he – he held me in his arms – and said. "Our baby," over and over – and then he said he would work so hard – for us both –'

'Do you want a boy or a girl?'

'It doesn't matter. Tom doesn't care, either, poor darling.' Her fingers plucked nervously at the sheet.

'What is it?' Sue asked her.

'Oh – Nurse Barton – I'm so worried about Tom. I – can hardly wait for the baby to come – but for – for Tom's sake I wish it – hadn't taken just this week – for arriving.'

'Why?'

'Well, you see, my husband is a fourth-year law student at Oxford. He – he's taking examinations – midyears – this week. It means so much to him to do well – and – how *can* he when he knows I'm here? He must be almost crazy, poor boy!'

'Goodness!' Sue had a vivid mental picture of the wretched law student.

In the slow hours of waiting Mrs Tom didn't once bemoan the fact that she was alone on this most important day of her life. She didn't worry about her condition from minute to minute, as most of the patients did. She thought only of Tom, and of the baby that was to be theirs so soon now. She babbled about the baby's clothes – she'd made every stitch of them herself, of the finest, softest material, and Tom had said – she quoted Tom at length. Poor Tom! What was he doing now?

Sue marvelled at the unselfishness of this girl, so little older than herself.

The baby came, late in the afternoon – a fat and healthy boy. His first cry would have done credit to a champion hog caller.

As that lusty bellow filled the little case room a look of ecstasy came into Mrs Tom's pale face. Her eyes, for a moment, seemed unearthly.

'Is – is – that – *my baby's voice?*' she stammered.

'That's what!' said the doctor. 'A fine boy!'

'*A boy!* Oh, please – *please* let me see my baby! Please let me hold him – just for one second! I *must!*' She was struggling upright – wildly.

'Here! Here! This won't do!' said the doctor. 'Give her the baby, Nurse Barton.'

Sue laid the fat, red nakedness in his mother's trembling arms.

Tears streamed down Mrs Tom's face. Her eyes searched the little face, feature by feature. Her shaking hands felt the sturdy little legs. 'My baby,' she whispered, '*at last!* My little son!' Dazed, she kissed the downy head, the pink fists, the wriggling toes, until, at a nod from the doctor, Sue wrapped the baby in a blanket and lifted him to the basket scales.

'Eight and a half pounds!'

Mrs Tom's eyes clung to the agitated basket.

'Tell Tom,' she murmured. 'He'll call – soon. Tell him – he has – a son!' She was asleep with the last word.

A week or two later Sue encountered a situation that was in startling contrast to this, and in which she played no small part.

The patient, this time, was a banker's wife. She

gave her age as forty, though she looked younger. She was a stately woman who, Sue thought, must be very handsome when she was in a good temper.

But she was not in a good temper, and neither was her husband. He came with her to the hospital – a tall, well-groomed man, with an assured manner. They made no attempt to conceal the reason for their unpleasant state of mind.

They didn't want a baby.

They didn't like children, had never wanted any, and why, now, in their middle years, should their settled way of life be disrupted by a child? They had planned a vacation in Italy for this winter. Now they couldn't go. Mrs Grant had had to give up her club work and her bridge parties.

No, they hadn't chosen a name for the baby. They didn't care what its name was. They didn't want to think about the baby. They hated it. No, Mrs Grant didn't know what baby clothes were in the suit-case. Her sister got some things for the baby yesterday. Mrs Grant hadn't looked at them herself.

Mr Grant had reserved the best room in the hospital for his wife. His flowers had been sent that morning, so that the room should be filled with them when she came.

Mrs Grant clung to him for a moment before she went to the case room. Her face was bitter. His was sullen.

When the baby was born Mrs Grant refused to look at it. She turned her face to the wall and waited grimly for the stretcher that would take her back to her room, making no reply when the doctor told her that the baby was a girl.

Sue gathered the blanketed baby into her arms. Poor mite – unwanted – actually hated. What kind of life would it have – left to the mercy of servants, starved for affection, kept in the background? The whole thing was incredible – horrible. Whether the Grants wanted the baby or not, they had it. They had no right in the world to refuse it love and the proper attention. There ought to be a law about such things!

Sue's lovely young face grew flushed and sullen with anger.

Oddly enough, the baby was strikingly beautiful. She had clinging golden curls all over her head, violet eyes with long, thick lashes, and a pure white skin. There was no trace of the redness of the newborn baby.

Sue yearned over her. 'I wish they'd give her to me,' she thought. 'I'd love her!'

Mr Grant was waiting when they arrived downstairs.

His wife held out her arms to him and he bent and kissed her.

'Oh, *Jack!*' she quavered.

'Darling!' he said.

That was all. He didn't ask about the baby. He had no more interest in it than had his wife. They were absorbed in each other – in their life together. The baby was an intruder. She had no meaning for them; no reality.

During the first three days, when the baby could have only warm water and whey, and was kept in the nursery, Mrs Grant did not once speak of her. She was Sue's patient, and Sue, with increasing resentment, began to go to the nursery to look at Baby

Grant whenever she had a spare minute. The baby
was very good – she rarely cried, though she often lay
awake and quiet in her crib, staring at nothing with
her great violet eyes. 'She can't possibly know that
they don't want her,' Sue reassured herself again and
again – and did not believe her own thought.

The girl on duty in the nursery shared Sue's feeling.

'That man needs a good wallop!' she said to Sue, on
the second day. 'I stopped him in the corridor a little
while ago and asked him if he didn't want to see the
baby, and he said "NO" and slammed out of the front
door!'

Sue leaned on the crib, watching the baby, who was
awake, and quiet as usual. Her little hands curled and
uncurled.

Could anything be done to make the Grants feel
differently? It would be worth the effort, worth any
amount of effort! Sue pondered, discussed the matter
with the nursery nurse. They got out the baby's suit-
case and looked at the clothes provided by Mrs
Grant's sister – who had good taste, at any rate. The
baby clothes were expensive, simple, and handmade
– in Paris.

'Look,' Sue said, 'let me take Baby Grant out to her
battle-axe of a mother to-morrow, will you? I've got
an idea! And dress her in the prettiest things she's
got.'

'Surely – if you like – but it won't do a bit of
good.'

'I suppose not – but there's no harm in trying.'

Baby Grant was ready the next day at two o'clock.
She looked almost too exquisite to be real. Her curls
were a golden sheen on her little head. Her eyelashes

made violet shadows on the glowing pink of her round cheeks.

Sue arranged the daintily tucked dress with care and lifted the baby from the crib.

'Now then, my lovely sweet,' she said, 'we stand or fall.'

Mr Grant was in his wife's room. Sue had made sure of that before she came for the baby – but now that the moment had come she wished she were well out of the whole business. It was not going to be easy to face those two – with their unwanted child in her arms.

On the threshold of the Grants' room Sue paused, to be met by two pairs of hostile eyes. Mr Grant rose to his feet with stiff courtesy, but it was Mrs Grant who spoke – from her bed.

'Is – that IT?' she asked harshly.

'Yes.' Sue stepped over the threshold, thinking grimly. 'Well – here goes!' Then, unexpectedly, to Mr Grant, 'Would you hold the baby, please, while I get Mrs Grant ready?' She plumped the baby into his arms before he had time to avoid it.

He looked utterly terrified, and made an inarticulate sound of protest. Mrs Grant said nothing. Her lips were set in a thin hard line.

She fussed around the bed, taking as much time as possible, and watching Mr Grant out of the corner of her eye.

He was quite white, and stood clutching the baby as if she might explode at any moment. Sue made no move to come to his rescue, and presently, as the baby neither shrieked nor leapt from his arms, he relaxed a little. The shock in his eyes gave way to curiosity. He looked at the baby, distantly at first, as though it were something loathsome, then with real attention, bending over it, wondering and intent.

The baby flourished a tiny pink hand. Almost absently, Mr Grant took it in his and looked at it. Sue, watching, saw him flush a deep red, and then, suddenly, he smiled into his daughter's violet eyes.

Sue stepped aside and Mrs Grant looked up at her husband.

'Why – why, *Jack*!' she said in a startled voice. Then, abruptly, to Sue, 'Bring the baby here, please.'

Sue laid the baby in the hollow of Mrs Grant's arm – an arm which curved involuntarily to receive it.

There was an odd silence.

Mr Grant was looking at the baby. So was his wife. Their eyes met suddenly over the tiny golden head.

Mrs Grant turned to Sue.

'Nurse Barton – I – I thought all new babies were supposed to be red and ugly. This one – isn't.'

Sue smiled. 'Most of them are. But *your* baby is an exception. She's the most beautiful baby that has ever been born in this hospital. Everybody is excited about her.'

'*Really?*' Mrs Grant looked down. 'She – she *is* pretty, isn't she?'

Mr Grant stepped forward, and bending over, touched the baby's fist with a large forefinger.

'Look, Lily,' he said, 'at her little hands!'

'But look at her *hair*, Jack! Did you ever *see* –'

Their eyes met again, and this time they smiled, tremulous, astonished smiles.

'Elizabeth,' Mrs Grant murmured reflectively. 'Elizabeth Ann – after your mother, Jack.'

Sue backed hastily from the room.

13
The Unexpected Always Happens

Sue and Connie had the afternoon off.

There wasn't much to do. It seemed silly to go into town to a movie when they had a chance to be out of doors. They had been in to the hospital to see Kit the evening before and found her in the infirmary, grumpy and inhospitable, with a cold. Skating or tobogganing was out of the question, for ponds and hillsides were deep in the slush of a February thaw.

'Let's go for a nice long walk,' Connie suggested, with unusual determination. 'We can come back and have tea by the fire.'

'Postman's holiday,' said Sue, laughing. 'But if you don't mind outraging your feet, I don't.' She thought, 'Connie's got something on her mind. She wants to talk.'

Connie, however, made no revelations until they had tramped several miles. It was a raw, grey day with a threat of snow in the air, but the girls were too glad to be away from the smell of lysol, from hard floors and the constant drive of work, to mind slush and grey skies. They set out briskly, Sue in a comfortable old ski suit and Connie in short fur coat and tweed skirt. They scorned hats.

It wasn't until the early winter twilight began to

shut down that they ceased to chatter amiably, and fell silent. They had reached real country now, and the white roofs of farmhouses looked lonely in the blue dusk. Sue shivered and quickened her pace.

'What's the matter?' Connie asked. 'Cold? Want to go back?'

Sue shook her head. 'No. I just – those farms look so low in their minds, somehow. They give me the creeps!'

'But, Sue,' Connie exclaimed, 'how can you think that? No place as popping with life and everything as a farm can be low in its mind. I mean – they're homes. Maybe the people in them have a hard time – but they – they share things. They're working for something, and – and –'

'That's all very noble and nice,' Sue interrupted, 'but would you like living in one of them yourself?'

Connie raised limpid eyes to Sue's face. 'I'd adore it,' she said simply. 'I'd live – anywhere – if – if –' she faltered.

'If Phil were there?' Sue ventured.

'Yes.'

'You've got it badly, haven't you, Connie?'

'Awfully – it's worse than scarlet fever. It's – oh, Sue, everything's so rotten!'

'Rotten! but, Connie, why? Of course, if you're going to stand there and tell me to my face that you're afraid he doesn't love you –'

'No, it's not that. I'm pretty sure he does, but –'

'But what?'

The half-melted snow splashed under their feet, loud in the winter stillness. Connie stared straight ahead with frightened eyes.

'It's so idiotic,' she burst out at last. 'It seems to me that every time I turn around I trip over all that money. You see, Phil doesn't know about it. He thinks I'm – well, he just doesn't know about it, that's all. I didn't tell him at first. Why should I? And now – oh, Sue – now that I know him better – I know it will drive him away.'

'You mean you think he'll say, "Never shall it be said that a Saunders was dishonoured by having a wife with money!" and will walk out into the night, the way they do in the movies. That doesn't seem very sensible. And anyway, isn't it your father's money? I mean, it isn't yours personally.'

'Oh yes, it is,' Connie said drearily. 'My grandmother left me a million dollars in a trust fund. Try and get rid of *that*!'

Sue gasped.

'A – a *million* dollars! Oh, Connie – and you never – good heavens! Why didn't you tell us?'

'Why should I? I've spent enough time trying to forget it myself. I wanted to be like other girls. Nobody had to know here. But now I want Phil – and when he finds out about the money he'll simply run for his life.'

Connie was right, Sue thought. It would take a man with great courage and great faith in himself not to be afraid of marrying a girl who had a million dollars. It would be too easy for all the world to call him a rich woman's husband.

'It always comes out all right in the movies,' she said hopefully.

'Then pray that this is an extra-super feature,' Connie said.

Late that night, when Connie, relieved to have shared her burden, had fallen asleep, Sue lay awake in the other bed, staring at the ceiling. It would be wonderful to be as sure as Connie. She couldn't stand it to lose Phil. Real love, it seemed, made you feel that way.

'Only I don't have to worry about losing Bill,' Sue thought, confused. 'He'll always be there – dear, patient Bill. And there are so many other things I want to do. I can't seem to get around to thinking about being married. Oh, I *wish* I knew what I wanted.'

There seemed no present solution to her problem, and a day or two later a change of duty took her mind from it, temporarily. She and Francesca Manson were sent to the third-floor nursery, and plunged into the task of taking care of twenty-two babies – so sweet to hold, so charming to bathe, so soft and warm and wriggling.

They grunted with satisfaction when Sue's slim young hand smoothed powder over their backs. Even Francesca grinned as she worked over them.

How achingly sweet it would be to bathe one's own baby. And babies were a part of marriage!

'Oh dear,' Sue thought, 'there I go again – round and round in a circle – wanting everything – and nothing.'

The girls had two 'premies' in the nursery – babies born prematurely – which had to be kept in incubators, and fed drop by drop – 'every time you turn around,' Francesca complained.

Francesca didn't care for the babies, though she was amused by them. She was considered hard by the other nurses, and she admitted that she didn't like patients. But she was a quick and capable workers. She had come to training school to learn how to be an organizer of hospitals and medical units, and she endured the patients with very poor grace. So Sue took care of the premies, and loved it. She also took all the care of a baby whose back wasn't right, and who required very careful handling.

It was another baby, Baby Williams, however, who made trouble between Sue and Francesca – trouble which was to bring real havoc into Sue's life in a way that she never dreamed of.

Baby Williams had the most voracious appetite that the girls had ever encountered. No amount of food satisfied him. He was a handsome baby, round and pink, with plump jowls, a single dollop of a curl on the top of his head, and the voice of an ambulance siren.

Babies need a great deal of sleep, and they are easily disturbed by noise – a matter of no consequence to Baby Williams, who yelled incessantly. He not only wanted food, he wanted it all the time; and twenty-one babies, upset by the noise, screamed in protest.

After two days of this, an exasperated supervisor burst into the nursery.

'What's the matter up here?' she demanded. 'I've never heard so much noise in my life!'

The girls explained, and were outraged when the supervisor suggested that he might be wet, or have wind, or a pin pricking him somewhere.

Francesca replied stiffly that nothing ailed Baby Williams but appetite.

The supervisor looked at the square opening that

was Baby William's mouth. The sounds issuing from it were deafening.

'Give him two ounces of whey,' she ordered, and left the nursery.

Baby Williams gulped the whey and bellowed for more. After some hesitation, Sue gave it to him. It disappeared in record time.

'He's just a souse!' Francesca said crossly.

'What'll we do with him? He couldn't possibly hold another drop – he's practically bogged down, now.'

Francesca leaned on the crib and looked at Baby Williams. Her face was unpleasant. Baby Williams whooped and roared.

Before Sue could make any move to stop her, Francesca had picked him up, turned him over her arm, and placed a single, brisk spank on the seat of his diapers.

'Yawp!' said Baby Williams in a startled voice, and fell silent.

Francesca's mouth was grim as she put the baby back in his crib. He lay there, puffing with surprise, but otherwise quiet.

'Well, I guess that's that – the little nuisance!' Francesca said.

A choking wave of anger caught Sue by the throat. She was unable to speak for a moment. The spank was nothing. New babies, just born, got far worse smacks from the doctor. And something had to be done, for the sake of the other babies. The spank had worked, too. It was the grim brutality in Francesca's face which had thrown Sue completely off balance.

'What a rotten thing to do!' Sue got out, at last.

Francesca shrugged. 'Why?'

'Because,' said Sue hotly, 'you did it just so that *you* wouldn't have to listen to him squall! If you were any kind of a nurse you'd have tried to think of something else, first!'

'Why didn't you think of something else?'

'You didn't give me a chance!'

'All right – go ahead and report me!'

'I've no intention of reporting you, and you know it! But I'd like to go on record as saying that I don't think your hard-boiled line is either funny or intelligent. And I notice you always pick on somebody who can't hit back.'

Francesca laughed, maintaining her pose of indifference, but her eyes were as angry as Sue's.

Neither of the girls mentioned the incident again. Baby Williams seemed permanently impressed, and cried no more than the other babies. Sue and Francesca continued to work together with every outward appearance of amiability, doing good teamwork as before. But there was a shadow between them, and Sue felt vaguely on guard, though against what she did not know.

A week or so after the unpleasantness about Baby Williams, Sue came off duty one evening to find Connie in a state of delirious excitement. Her cap was over one ear; her cheeks were flushed; her eyes shone; and her delicate, nervous hands fluttered as she spoke.

'Sue! Oh, Sue! I'm – *engaged!*'

'Oh, Connie! I'm *so* glad! Congratulations, darling!' Sue caught the fluttering hands, and kissed Connie heartily.

'Look!' Connie drew her left hand from Sue's and

held it out. On the third finger was a tiny diamond, set in a pathetically meagre platinum band.

It would take Phil, Sue thought, quite a long time to pay for that – and Connie could have bought it with a day's allowance. Poor Phil!

'I know what you're wondering,' Connie said slowly. 'I – I haven't told him – yet. But I will. I haven't quite got the courage now.'

Sue was appalled. The longer Connie put it off the harder it would be – the more difficult to explain to Phil. But it was Connie's own business. 'I'd better get off the subject,' Sue thought. 'Let the poor kid be happy while she can.' Aloud she said, 'Of course, Connie. You know what you want to do. Come on, lamb, tell me all about it! About Phil, I mean. When did it happen, and where, and everything!'

Connie was only too thankful to forget the subject of money and return to her happiness. She talked eagerly, her words tumbling over one another. Sue pulled up a chair and pushed her into it, and listened.

Phil had come out unexpectedly that afternoon, so grave and sweet and sort of flustered. Connie couldn't go out with him because she was on call for the case room, but they had had the living-room to themselves. It had all happened there – 'in that blessed, cramped, chintzy little room!'

'He said,' Connie bubbled, 'that he couldn't wait any longer – he had to know – the dear idiot – as if the way I felt about him wouldn't be plain even to the babies in the nursery. We got all mixed up, and laughed, and cried a little – at least I did – and it was all too – too – oh, well, why go into it?'

'What about your family?' Sue asked.

Connie shrugged, with a bitterness very unlike her. 'Mother doesn't care what I do,' she said. 'She's given me up as hopeless.' Her face lighted again. 'But Dad will be pleased. He only wants me to be happy.'

'When are you going to be married?'

Connie's happiness fled instantly. She was silent for a moment. Then she said wretchedly, 'Phil is planning on it in a few months after I graduate. He's going to get a – a rise pretty soon. But I – I'm not planning *anything*. You'll – probably see me walking down the aisle in an empty – church – singing the – the "Wedding March" off key – and all by myself – while Phil will be that – big cloud of dust – over the horizon.'

'Connie! *Don't!*' Sue cried.

It was all a horrid mess, Sue thought. She got the happy and miserable Connie to bed at last and dropped off to sleep herself, feeling that the older one grew the more confusing things became.

Connie, in the next week, did nothing to lessen this opinion. She was alternately wildly happy and utterly miserable and frightened. She went out with Phil evening after evening, to return white and tense. She sobbed in her sleep. She sprang out of bed in the morning, singing. She turned white suddenly at the dinner table and didn't answer when spoken to. Something, Sue thought, was going to happen before long.

Something did – but not to Connie.

Sue was bathing babies one morning, receiving them from Francesca, who did the weighing and charting. One of the babies had had a mild attack of colic, which had delayed their schedule, and they were working rapidly and silently in an effort to make

up lost time and get the babies downstairs by nine
o'clock.

Sue, absorbed in scrubbing, drying, and powdering, was unaware that Francesca was looking at her
from time to time with her odd, one-sided smile.

When the last baby had been handed over,
Francesca remarked casually, 'I was in town yesterday. I went over to the hospital.'

'Mmmm,' Sue murmured, and lathered a small,
fuzzy head, smiling as the baby squeaked.

'There's a lot of talk going around about Eleanor
Gerard and Bill Barry.'

The sponge slipped from Sue's hand into the water.
She picked it up instantly, but Francesca's quick eyes
had seen, and her thin lips curved into their twisted
smile.

'Really?' said Sue.

'Yes – really. Anyway, the talk is real enough; of
course, the place is always full of rumours. But
everybody knows that she's been crazy about him for
ages – and she's the kind who gets her man.'

'Well –' Sue's voice sounded strange and far away.
She cleared her throat carefully. 'I wouldn't think
she'd have to sit up nights planning how to do that –
she's one of the stunningest little models I've ever
seen.' She lifted the dripping baby to the towel on her
lap, and bent over it.

Francesca, leaning against a crib, waited until Sue
looked up to reach for a pledget of cotton. Then she
dropped her bomb.

'As a matter of fact,' she said, 'there is something in
the talk that they go out together all the time –
because I saw them myself last night, coming out of
the Majestic Theatre – arm in arm.'

There was a stunned silence of fully thirty seconds. Francesca smiled again, watching the colour drain from Sue's face. Sue recovered herself – with what effort only she could know. Her voice shook a little, in spite of its lightness of tone.

'Oh, well,' she said, 'girls will be girls – but isn't it rather careless of them to be seen in so public a place? Miss Mason might have picked that night to go to the theatre.'

'Gerard wouldn't care. She'd think the game was worth the candle.'

'In that case – why worry?' Sue pulled a flannel petticoat over the baby's head, and reached for a tiny dress.

Francesca laughed. 'Goodness! *I'm* not worrying.'

The baby was ready now. Sue tucked it under her arm and stood up. 'There!' she said. 'They're done! Shall I take them down or will you?'

'Oh, you go ahead. You like doing it. Unless, of course, you don't feel up to it. You – er – don't look very well. Is anything the matter?'

Sue took refuge, blindly, in an old gag. 'Something I ate, no doubt.'

She opened the elevator door, and wheeled the truckload of babies inside. The elevator rattled slowly downward. Sue thought, 'I must look carefully at their tags. I mustn't give the wrong babies to the right mothers – no, I mean I mustn't –' Irrelevant words, fragments of sentences, swirled dizzily around in her mind, but the business of getting out the babies steadied her at last.

There was a curious, sharp pain in her chest, as if something heavy were crushing it. That was odd, too, because she didn't seem to be thinking any thoughts with *feeling*. There was just that pain. She waited quietly beside the truck until the babies should be ready again. Once she pressed her hand against her chest. She was thinking clearly now.

There was no reason why Bill shouldn't go out with other girls, and if it were anyone but Bill the fact would have no significance. But Bill wasn't a chaser; he was too wrapped up in his work. He would never waste time in playing around. If he took a girl out, or paid her definite attention, it meant just one thing – he was becoming seriously interested in that girl.

It was her own fault, Sue thought heavily. She'd diddled around – acted like a fourteen-year-old child – didn't know what she wanted – kept him dangling. He was tired of it – probably disgusted and out of patience.

'I've been in love with him all along, and didn't know it. *But I know now* – and it's too late! I've lost him! He'd never do that – if I hadn't!' She saw his dear, dark head, outlined in moonlight, with the chimes singing through the night above it. He'd asked her to marry him. He'd offered her all that he had, or was, or hoped to be – and she'd temporized – dodged the issue – rewarded him with a chilly kiss after she'd flung his offer back at him.

This was being in love – this pain. It was knowing that nothing else was important – none of those other things. What was it she'd thought she'd wanted? Had *he* hurt like this – because of her? 'Oh, Bill – my *dear*!' She'd thought he was *always* going to be around – hurting! How did you make the pain stop? How did you get away from it?

'Hey! Barton!' said a voice. 'Wake up, m'love. It's daytime and all the little birds are awake. Were you going to take the babies back, or have you moved the nursery down here?'

'What? Oh! Sorry!'

Well, you could always work. That might help.

14
Another Shock

Sue struggled awake to the familiar pain. It had become a dull, steady ache, and it was always there. She was conscious of it, waking, even before she remembered its cause.

'Barton! *Telephone!*'

'All right – be right down,' Sue called, groping for bathrobe and slippers. *Could* it be Bill? He called her up sometimes – not often. Sue's heart began to pound.

The room was greying in the early spring twilight. Sue glanced at the other bed. Connie was still asleep. It was Kit on the telephone, of course. It – it *wouldn't* be Bill. Sue fumbled for the doorknob and ran down the stairs, pulling her bathrobe around her. The telephone booth was in the hall, and whoever yelled up the stairs had vanished.

Sue snatched up the receiver.

'Hello?'

'Hello!' said a man's voice. 'Sue Barton?'

'Yes – speaking,' said Sue, weak with disappointment.

'This is George Lamson. I wondered if you were doing anything to-night. I thought – perhaps –'

'I'm terribly sorry – I'm on night duty.' She was thankful for that. Even if there had been no risk involved, she didn't want to go out with Lamson.

What had struck him to call her up after all this time?
Somebody else had failed him, probably.

'Gee – that's too bad,' he said. 'I've got a nice shiny
new car – came to-day – and I wanted to show it off. I
could have you back by ten.'

'I'm sorry,' Sue repeated patiently. 'I'm on nights,
and we don't have an eight-hour day here. We go on
at seven.'

'Well – I guess that settles that.'

'I'm afraid it does. How are you?'

'Oh, fine – burnishing up my shield to dazzle
probationers.' There was a pause. 'Oh, by the way,
I've some news for you. Bill Barry left the hospital
to-day. There's a rumour he's resigned. Anyway,
Parker is taking his place – but I don't know whether
it's permanent or not, and neither does Parker. Hello
– hello – are you still there?'

'Yes.' Sue tried to speak clearly above the tightness
in her throat. 'Yes. I heard you. How –' Her voice
stopped working. She tried again. 'How does it
happen Parker is taking his place? Aren't you senior
to Parker?'

'No – he's nearer through than I am. Sure you
wouldn't have time for even a short drive?'

'No – I really couldn't.'

'O.K. How about –'

'I'm afraid I have to go now. Someone's calling me.
But thanks a lot for asking me. Good-night.'

'Good-night.'

So that was why he had called – or was it? It didn't
matter. Bill gone – and without a word to her. Oh – he
wouldn't do that. They were still friends at least.
Perhaps he'd written.

Sue was at the mail rack in one bound. There was no letter and she went slowly and heavily upstairs. 'I don't believe I can stand much more,' she thought dully. Bill had left the hospital! It couldn't be – but it was. She'd be through at James Memorial in one more week – she'd go back, and Bill wouldn't be there. It was impossible!

His letter came the next day in the three o'clock post. Sue, hollow-eyed from lack of sleep, was waiting for it. She'd gone downstairs for the eleven o'clock post, and after that she dressed and tried to read, but the words blurred before her eyes.

Now it had come and she could only stare at it stupidly. After a while, holding it unopened in her hand, she went into the tiny living-room and sat down in a corner. The corner was partly cut off by a screen from the rest of the room, and Sue was quite unconscious of having selected it because it seemed, somehow, protective.

She opened the letter at last.

It was dated the day before.

DEAR SUE [she read], –
    I tried to get you on the telephone this noon, but they said you were sleeping and could not be disturbed.

'Oh!' Sue cried aloud, out of the depths of bitterness.

I didn't have a chance to telephone you again. I've been called away, suddenly, on a matter of business. There isn't anything to tell you about it, yet. It's too uncertain. I don't know how long I'll be gone – several months, probably. If everything turns out as I expect, I shall resign from my job

in the hospital – but I'll know more about that later. For the
present I have a three months' leave of absence.

I'm sorry not to see you before I go, but there is no time.
If you would care to write me, my address will be 31
Montgomery St., Springdale, New Hampshire.

Best of luck to you, Sue. Sincerely,

BILL.

That was all. A stiff letter, saying nothing. He was
sorry not to see her before he left, but there was no
time. He could have *made* time if he'd *wanted* to see
her. But of course he didn't – now. Sue's hands,
holding the letter, lay nerveless in her lap.

Bill was gone. It was strange that everything didn't
stop. The worn screen beside her kept on standing
there. The March dusk was shutting down on the
hospital as usual, making grey squares of the
window-panes. Everything was the same, and
nothing would ever be the same again. Even the
doorbell, ringing in the hall, had a different sound.

Sue heard a quick thud of steps on the stairs. That
was Connie's voice telling somebody to come in –
Phil, probably. Poor Connie – Sue had scarcely been
aware of her these last two weeks.

They'd come in here. Sue couldn't see anybody
now. She was utterly lifeless – sodden with despair. If
she were eavesdropping it was against her will. She
had no wish to hear, but she couldn't move. And
anyway, what difference did it make? She'd sit here
quietly, behind the screen, and wait until they'd gone.

There was an eddy of movement in the room and
then a brief silence. They didn't sit down, because
nothing creaked.

Phil's grave young voice said, 'Darling, I just got

your note, and I came as quickly as I could. Has anything happened?'

Connie's shaken, frightened voice said: 'Not – exactly, Phil. I've something – to tell you. I – I've been trying to for days when we've been together – but I couldn't. I had to – to make a special –'

'What *is* it, sweet?'

'You know I love you, Phil, don't you?'

'And I love you – more than anything in the world. Tell me what's the matter!'

'Then please listen – and don't interrupt – because if you do I – won't be able to tell you – and I've got to! Phil – I – should have said this – before – but I *couldn't!* Oh, Phil – I –' Sue heard a long breath. 'Phil, I'm not – poor – the way you thought – the way I let you think. I've got a – a million dollars.'

There was a long silence.

'Phil?' Connie said timidly.

And then the room echoed to his astonishing laughter.

'*Phil!*'

'I'm sorry, darling,' Phil said, sobering at once. 'I didn't mean to be – raucous – but you frightened me so, Connie dear. I – I thought you were going to tell me you'd stopped loving me – or something.'

'Oh,' Connie said. 'Then it doesn't matter?'

'A million dollars,' Phil said at last, 'always matters.' There was a grin in his voice again. 'Think of all the telephone calls you can make, and all the trolleys you can ride on! It's a very solemn thought.'

'Then everything isn't all changed with us?'

The laughter went out of Phil's voice. He weighed his words, speaking carefully.

'My dear,' he said, 'there's no use pretending I don't know what you mean. You're afraid I won't be able to endure the fact that people will think you're keeping me in silk shirts and fancy garters.' He paused. 'Well, all my friends know that I don't wear silk shirts – and that I can really keep myself in fancy garters. I hope you won't mind living in the sort of apartment I can afford. I hope you won't mind having only the one maid I can pay for. As for the rest – darling, it's your money. Do what you like. Buy yourself a horse car, or a couple of rubies stolen from a Hindu idol. Just keep on loving me – that's all I ask.'

'You darling – fool!'

It seemed a long time before they went away, but at last the front door closed and Connie's steps were feather-light on the stairs.

Sue remained where she was, motionless.

This was what she might have had.

The room was quite dark now. Outside, the pines were black arrows against the sky, and small spring stars tangled in their branches. A gust of wind shook the house, and far away across some valley an owl hooted.

She stood up, slowly and stiffly. She must dress; she must eat something; she must go on duty.

15
Last Months

Sue was glad to be back in her own hospital again. It was strange that one could be glad and unhappy at the same time. But the hospital was home. She had loved it for a long time and she still loved it. It steadied her with familiarness.

She was alone a great deal in her off-duty time, now. Kit had gone to James Memorial the day that Sue and Connie had returned. Connie was out with Phil in all her spare moments, and Sue had never been on particularly intimate terms with the other nurses.

Connie worried about Sue's thinness, and brought back offerings of food – fruit, ice-cream, sandwiches. Sue ate them and remained thin. Connie was too sensitive to try to force a confidence and, as Sue offered none, she asked no questions. She and Phil begged Sue to go out with them, and she went occasionally because she was touched by their solicitude and didn't wish to be ungracious.

She met Miss Cameron in the corridor one day, and after a glance at her Miss Cameron snapped, 'You're all points! What's the matter with you?'

'Nothing, Miss Cameron, thank you.'

'Nonsense! Your colour is bad – very bad! I shall speak to Miss Mason!'

She did – with the result that Sue was ordered to report to the Emergency Ward, where a thorough physical examination revealed nothing wrong, and the prescription of a vile tonic only added to Sue's misery.

She was sent, for duty, to the Private Pavilion, a section of the hospital reserved for the very rich, and here she got still another angle on human nature. The rich, she found, were more frightened by sickness than were the poor, but they were usually in better spirits.

They complained more, but in the midst of their complaints would pause to describe a major catastrophe so wittily that it brought tears of laughter to the eyes of the listener.

Duty in the Private Pavilion was usually of three months' duration, and Sue, happy at being anywhere in the hospital, settled down to the familiar routine.

April came with its soft skies and swelling buds. The ivy vines put out tiny new leaves, and sudden rains streaked the hospital windows with silver. Sue was making up classes missed at James Memorial, and was working hard. There wasn't much time for brooding over her woes and presently she found that the dull pain – the feeling that something heavy was crushing her chest – had gone away, leaving in its place a quite bearable melancholy.

'I suppose,' she thought, realizing this, 'that nobody can go on hurting like that for ever. You couldn't stand it.'

On the first of May Connie went to the Amphitheatre for her course in anæsthetics, a fact which gave Sue a slight feeling of frustration – all that beautiful training to end in Connie's being married. Though, of course, one never knew when such a thing might be useful – even if one were married.

Toward the middle of the month a brief note came from Bill. He had resigned from the hospital. There was much to be done in Springdale. He was enjoying it.

Sue wondered dully what he wrote to Eleanor Gerard, though she couldn't seem to feel that it mattered any more.

She answered his letter. It was June before he replied, and she almost wished that he would stop writing and let her alone, to forget him if she could.

She gathered from his letter that he was doing a great deal of operating, but where or why he did not say. He mentioned that June in New Hampshire was cold; there was still frost in the mornings. He missed the hospital. He asked if her home wasn't somewhere in his vicinity. He hoped that she wasn't getting too tired.

At the end of two weeks Sue replied – carefully, as before – a brief, friendly little note.

He didn't answer that at all, but in the middle of July she had a surprising letter from her mother.

. . .Such a nice young man called on us last Sunday – a Dr Barry. He said he knew you in the hospital. Your father liked him so much – and that's unusual with Dad. They went off together, poking around the place and laughing. I hope Dad didn't bore him with all the details of how he grafted his pear trees. Ted is well and sends love. . . .

It was nice of Bill to call on her family, but why bother? He didn't have to be friendly to that extent. Oh, well . . .

Kit was back now from the James Memorial and Sue was less lonely. They went canoeing on hot July nights, as they had done in the years before. Sometimes Connie went with them, and once or twice brought Phil.

Kit, like Connie, made no effort to extract confidences from Sue.

It was odd, Sue thought, that Kit didn't fall in love with somebody. Sue had a vague notion that Kit was interested in a man at home, but wasn't sure about it. Anyway, the house officers all liked her, and if she didn't go out with them it wasn't for lack of invitations.

Kit, herself, commented on this once.

'It's so sweet of them,' she remarked sarcastically, 'the dear, generous souls – "Do come out and entertain us, and if you get into trouble because of it we'll feel too, too terribly." Phooey!'

Sue laughed. She was feeling almost like herself again. 'Maybe I'm getting over him,' she thought with relief.

The first of August, ushered in with a heat wave and thunderstorms, found Sue a staff nurse. She had almost forgotten her talk with Miss Waring and the resulting determination to try being an executive – if the Office were willing.

The Office, it seemed, had decided without any prompting to give her that opportunity.

'We're going to put you in charge of Ward 29,' Miss Mason said, pinning the half-inch-wide band of black velvet to Sue's cap. 'We believe that you have executive ability, and will make a good staff nurse.'

She had thought that she would never feel anything again, but she left the Officer walking on air. Ward 29 was men's convalescent, and an easy ward – but it was a *ward*, and she was its staff nurse! As she hurried up the incline past the X-ray rooms she saw Hilda Grayson coming down, and she tried with very poor success to appear nonchalant.

Hilda stopped short half-way down the incline.

'Barton!' she shrieked, and then clapped her hand over her mouth. 'Barton! You're a *staff nurse!* When did it happen? What ward? Why –'

'Ward 29,' Sue replied as calmly as she could. 'Just now. I'm going up this minute to – to take – charge.'

'Oh, Bat! How marvellous! Congratulations!' She grinned suddenly. 'Wait till Willie hears about this! Oh, look at your cunning black band! I – wish – I had one!'

'Well, I'll bet you will before long.' Sue tried hard not to be triumphant – but it *was* pretty marvellous! And the little black band, she thought, as she went on, was the last step before the broad black band of the graduate nurse. This duty would probably be her last in the hospital, for student nurses usually remained in charge of their wards from three to four months. Graduation was only a month and a half away, and the two months Sue must make up after it would undoubtedly be made up while she was in charge of 29.

Sue had still another reason for being excited, however. Like all student nurses, she had thought many times that *she* could run a ward far better than most of the staff nurses for whom she had worked. *She* would never set her nurses a task and then interrupt them before it was finished. She would never sit idly at her desk while the girls worked – she'd work herself, with them. They should have exactly the off-duty time they wanted, and if they stopped to talk sometimes she wouldn't nag at them – she'd understand. She wouldn't make these changes at first, of course; she'd introduce them gradually, and the Office would wake up some day to discover that Ward 29's staff nurse was practically a genius.

This was all very fine, but it was not as easy to put into practice as Sue had expected. There was more to running a ward then she had thought, and her plans for making it a heaven for nurses got mislaid while she was learning how to order food for twenty-five patients, medical supplies for the ward, special diets, the proper amount of laundry. She must make rounds with house officers, staff surgeons, supervisors. She must see that the house officer wrote his orders instead of giving them verbally. She must supervise the maid's work. The ward must be kept clean. All doctors' orders must be carried out exactly. Complaints of patients must be attended to with firmness and tact. Patients must be kept comfortable and happy and well-cared-for. All the work must be done according to schedule and on time.

Under these circumstances it was difficult not to interrupt the nurses' work, but at the end of two weeks Sue decided that she had the ward sufficiently well in hand to try a few experiments.

The general work of the ward was divided equally among her four nurses. There was a dish nurse in charge of the kitchen and meals; there was a medicine and linen nurse, a laboratory and laundry nurse, a nurse who attended to the ten-o'clock and three-o'clock 'nourishment.' They were all busy at their particular tasks when Sue remembered that the patient McCarthy must be sent to X-ray at ten-fifteen. Well, she'd go with him herself.

When she returned to the ward she found that the supervisor, two staff surgeons, and the house officer had been there in her absence and that the supervisor had been extremely annoyed to find Sue gone.

A day or two later Sue tried her plan of working around the ward instead of sitting at the desk. Miss Masters, the supervisor, found her in the linen closet, stacking towels and pillow-cases on the shelves.

'What's all this, Miss Barton?'

Sue explained. The nurses were rushed, and she had thought –

The supervisor was pleasant but firm.

'Stacking linen is the work of your nurses, Miss Barton. You cannot keep all the reins of a busy ward in your hands unless you are where you can see what is going on – and the linen closet is not the place for it. If the work on the ward is so badly arranged that the staff nurse must do some of it herself – then *she is not a good executive!*'

'Yes, Miss Masters.'

Sue followed the white uniform into the ward. The supervisor went to the desk, checked over the day's requisitions for supplies, and glanced at the time slip.

'But, Miss Barton!' she exclaimed. 'You can't send in a time slip like that. You'll be left with only one nurse to get out the suppers to-night.'

'I'm sorry, Miss Masters. Miss Allison asked especially for that time off, and I thought –'

'What Miss Allison wants is of no consequence if it conflicts with the needs of the ward. Never make out a time slip like that again, Miss Barton.'

'Very well, Miss Masters. Thank you.'

So here was an end to Sue's happy ideas of making the ward a blissful place for her nurses. Her student point of view was undergoing some rapid changes.

There were other problems.

A new house officer, fresh from medical school, had come to the ward, full of notions and importance. His schemes, if carried out, would have disrupted the ward. He had no idea of ward routine, or of the fact that routine was essential to the well-being of the patients. He wished to change the hour for doing dressings from nine in the morning to eleven – which meant that all the beds must be made a second time. He inaugurated a fancy system of charting which required a great deal of time. He wanted not only a dressing nurse to assist him, but Sue as well.

Sue made the mistake of combating this too vigorously, and there was an unpleasant scene. The matter was finally laid before the senior house officer and Miss Masters, who explained to the young doctor that the hospital had not been founded for his especial benefit, and that present methods had been found to be quite adequate. The house officer, in consequence, felt frustrated and resentful, and complained that Sue would not co-operate with him.

Sue learned tact from this experience, and for a time everything went smoothly.

Then she was sent a new nurse, one of the younger students – a Nurse Taffereau. The girl was almost too young, Sue thought. She had very little sense of responsibility, and, though her prettiness and bright remarks amused the men, she was of very little value otherwise. Her beds were badly made. Crumbs were left in her patients' sheets at night. She forgot things. She shirked.

Sue struggled with her patiently, and Nurse Taffereau was always so sorry – she didn't mean – she thought – and Nurse Allison had told her to leave those things in the laboratory.

Miss Allison, when questioned, very obviously knew nothing of the matter.

When it became Nurse Taffereau's turn for relief duty. Sue was worried. She had misgivings about leaving the ward solely in the hands of this pretty, irresponsible youngster from seven until eleven at night. But she could not, in fairness, give the other nurses extra relief duty. Nurse Taffereau would have to learn.

Nurse Taffereau accepted her relief duty with alacrity and Sue was a little astonished. She had not expected so lively a person to be pleased at giving up all her evenings for a week.

It was on the third evening of Nurse Taffereau's relief duty that Sue remembered, about nine o'clock, that her book on psychology was on the ward. If she ran over and got it now she'd have time for an hour's study before lights-out.

She went by the back stairs, because they were nearest, and opened the ward door very quietly. It was early for patients to be asleep, but it was time they were settling for the night, and comings and goings were disturbing.

The only light in the ward was over the desk at the far end. There was no sign of Nurse Taffereau. She was probably setting up trays in the kitchen.

Sue closed the door silently behind her and stood

leaning against it, looking with pride at her neat ward. Scarcely realizing that she was doing so, she ran a finger along the shutter of the window beside her – and felt a powdering of dust. She must be more firm with the maid than she had been – *what was that?*

Whatever it was had come from the third bed on the right. It might have been a sound. It might have been a movement. Sue was not sure which it was, but instinct told her that something was wrong. She strained her eyes through the dimness and for a moment thought that handsome eighteen-year-old Eddie was trying to get out of bed. His hip was in a cast, and he mustn't – she'd speak to him at once!

Sue took a step forward and then halted – stunned, incredulous.

Nurse Taffereau was sitting in a chair close beside Eddie's bed, and as Sue looked the boy flung out a careless arm, pulled down the young nurse's head – and kissed her!

Sue stood rigid, completely without thought, her mind unable to function from pure shock. Then, slowly, a thought emerged. 'Go outside. Do nothing until you've had time to think. Go outside.'

She turned and went silently out into the hall, closing the door behind her.

What ought she to do?

Eddie was a perfectly nice boy – harum-scarum and full of life. Miss Taffereau was just a pretty, silly kid. They were two foolish youngsters. If Eddie weren't a *patient* – if they weren't in the hospital – but he was – and they were!

Sue rubbed a shaking hand across her temples. As staff nurse, if she took official notice of the scene it must be official notice – and that meant that she must report Miss Taffereau to the Training School Office. If she did that, Miss Taffereau would certainly be expelled – and Sue would be responsible. She would be a squealer!

Two years and a half of training had taught Sue exactly what the school thought of squealers.

It would be very easy to slip away and no one need ever know that she had seen. But then Miss Taffereau would go right on doing this kind of thing, and if she weren't stopped, would graduate and go out to give the whole nursing profession a bad name.

Sue was a head nurse. She was responsible for the behaviour of the nurses on her ward. Could she let this go? Suppose one of the other patients had seen – what kind of reputation would the *school* have when he went out and told? What would Eddie have to say to his friends about nurses? No, the school was more important than any one nurse in it, and in the entire period of her training Sue had never before known of a nurse who had other than professional relations with a patient. Maybe things like that could happen in other schools, but not in this one. Oh, *no*, not in this one – the finest training school in the country! It was unthinkable. It *couldn't* happen – but it had!

And yet – could she ruin the girl's career?

That, unhappily, was the answer. The fact that the Office would consider the offence serious enough for expulsion told Sue what she must do.

'But I won't sneak!' she told herself firmly. 'It's going to be dreadful for Taffereau, and I can at least take my share of the unpleasantness by facing her first.'

She opened the door and went into the ward.

Miss Taffereau rose and came forward confidently.

Sue drew her out into the corridor and told the girl what she had seen.

The nurse's face went white. Furious with terror, she said, '*It's not true! I didn't!*'

'But I saw you,' Sue said quietly.

'You're lying! You sneaked up here to spy on me! You've never liked me, and now you're trying to get me thrown out!'

'I'm sorry. I don't want to report you – but I must. You – you don't understand. You can't do a thing like this to – to nurses – to the school.'

'Oh, the school! The school! Always the school! I'm sick to death of it! A lot of sneaks always picking on you!'

'I'm sorry,' Sue repeated and, turning, went slowly and miserable down the stairs.

'I hope you're satisfied!' Miss Taffereau screamed after her.

It was a ghastly business.

The night supervisor sent for Miss Taffereau at once. There were denials and tears in the Office. The night supervisor stood by Sue – who almost wished she wouldn't.

'We have never had occasion to doubt Miss Barton's word, Miss Taffereau, and we have never known her to be vindictive. We have been watching you for a long time, and your work has been far from satisfactory. I am very sorry that this has happened, for your sake as well as for the hospital's, and Miss Matthews will be very much distressed.'

Miss Matthews, called from her room, came over at

once, and there was something in her face, as she listened to the supervisor's recital, which frightened Miss Taffereau.

Miss Matthews turned to the girl at last, her eyes like polished steel. She spoke slowly and distinctly.

'You are very young Miss Taffereau, and if this were your first offence, even such an offence as this, I would be willing to give you another chance. But your work has been consistently careless. You have been lazy, indifferent, and irresponsible. I have spoken to you about this before, if you remember. It has done no good.' She paused a moment, her broad, kindly face suddenly old.

'You are relieved from duty, Nurse Taffereau. I shall expect you to have left the school by nine o'clock to-morrow morning. I will write to your parents – and I would advise you to take up some other line of work. Nursing is not a suitable profession for you.'

'I'm leaving right now!' Nurse Taffereau stormed. 'And glad of it!'

'That will do. You may go.'

Nurse Taffereau went.

'Miss Barton,' Miss Matthews said gently, 'this has been a very difficult thing for you to do. I want you to know that we fully realize the fact.'

Sue spend a sleepless night, and in the morning was prepared to face the scorn of the entire school. She had been a squealer. To her amazement the school knew nothing of the affair, and neither Sue nor the school ever saw Miss Taffereau again.

It was almost a week before information filtered through the school that that little Taffereau snippet had left – sickness at home was rumoured to be the cause.

Sue broke down in the end, and confessed to Kit and Connie. They listened, wide-eyed and shocked.

'You did exactly right,' Kit said, when Sue had finished. 'That's not squealing! It means something to be a graduate of this hospital – that's why I came here – but it wouldn't be for long, if that kind stayed in it.'

'But the poor kid,' Sue began. 'She's just a little idiot –'

'Well, let her be an idiot somewhere else, then.'

'And don't worry about Taffereau,' Connie said 'She'll get on!'

'I suppose so,' Sue agreed, 'but I don't think I like being an executive after all. That kid is going to haunt me. I'll wake up in the night having fits and all that. If this is execking, give me a nice peaceful hornet's nest!'

16
New Plans

Sue answered the telephone herself.

Miss Mason's voice said, 'Miss Matthews would like to see you in her office, Miss Barton, if you can leave the ward.'

'Yes, Miss Mason. I'll be right down.'

Sue hung up and went in search of her ward senior.

'Miss Allison,' she said, in what she hoped was a casual and far from nervous voice, 'I'm leaving the ward for a few minutes.' It was one of the advantages of being a head nurse that you didn't have to explain your movements – not to the students, anyway.

'Yes, Miss Barton.'

Sue hurried down the long, winding stone stairs. Her knees didn't feel as weak as they would have felt a year ago at such a summons, but they were weak enough. Why should *Miss Matthews* want to see her? If the Office had found out about her and Kit coming in late the other night, and skipping past the maid without signing the pass book – surely Miss Mason would attend to that matter.

It might be her room – she'd left it in rather a mess. But there, again, one of the other supervisors would speak to Sue – Miss Matthews had no time for such minor matters. It couldn't be anything on the ward, or Miss Masters would have had something to say before now. And it wasn't about – Bill – because there wasn't anything to be – and he'd been gone nearly six months, anyway.

Sue felt her cap. It was on straight, as nearly as she could tell. Her bib and apron were spotless. Her cuffs were clean. She had no buttons missing.

The air in the rotunda was cool against her flushed face, but across the curving expanse was that frightening door, coming nearer with every step. Sue's middle felt like jelly.

'Stop it, Sue Barton!' she told herself. 'You're a senior – graduating this very month. You can't go around acting like a piece of wet seaweed!'

She halted at the threshold of Miss Matthews's office.

Miss Matthews was sitting at her desk, her stout figure in its white uniform sharply outlined against the window. Sue noticed with real dismay that there were grey strands in Miss Matthews's brown hair.

'I wonder if we've done that to her?' Sue thought, realizing, for the first time, that the position of Superintendent of Nurses in a large hospital was not the life of ease and power it was popularly supposed to be.

Sue knocked on the casing.

Miss Matthews looked up, and her broad, high-cheek-boned face expanded in a warm smile.

'Come in, Miss Barton, and sit down.'

Sue took the indicated chair, sitting gingerly on its edge. She would not have been in the least surprised if it had exploded under her.

Miss Matthews leaned back in her chair and looked reflectively at the flushed young face before her, seeing it, perhaps, not as Sue Barton, but as a composite of a thousand other young faces, scattered now all across the world.

'Miss Barton,' she said at last, 'have you decided what you want to do when you graduate?'

So *that* was it! Sue breathed again.

'No, I haven't, Miss Matthews.'

'Would you be interested in remaining here in your present position?'

Sue had a momentary throb of elation. They wanted her to stay on! She *had* been a good head nurse! How simply gorgeous! But it wouldn't do. She didn't want to be an executive. She wanted to take care of patients, lots of them. Sue thought carefully before she replied.

'No, Miss Matthews, thank you. I – I don't think I like executive work very much. I like – patients.'

Miss Matthews smiled. 'We know that you do, Miss Barton. And I'm glad you realize it. There is a special field for young women like you.'

Sue looked at her, puzzled. Surely she didn't mean private nursing.

'I refer to Public Health work – to District Nursing, Miss Barton. It is one of the most important branches of nursing, and the work in it has scarcely begun. I believe that you are unusually fitted for such work, and I would suggest that you take a special course in it – at the Henry Street Settlement, in New York – or elsewhere, if you prefer.'

Sue was thinking fast. Public Health work! She should have known it herself! In city slums she would be doing exactly the kind of thing she loved – she'd be taking care of lots and lots of patients who would need what she could give them more than almost any patients in the world. They would have to be taught how to take care of themselves and their children – and Sue liked teaching. Their living conditions were awful. A nurse could do *something* about that.

Miss Matthews, who was watching Sue's face, smiled again.

'I thought you would feel that way about it,' she said quietly.

Sue looked up. 'It's just the right thing for me, isn't it?' she said. 'I – I'd love to do that kind of work.'

Sue left the office bubbling with excitement. At the door Miss Matthews's voice stopped her.

'Oh – er – Miss Barton – when you come in late please sign the – er – pass book. The maid isn't as nimble as she used to be.'

'Yes, Miss Matthews.'

Sue was grinning broadly when she crossed the rotunda. If anyone had eyes that could see around corners, Miss Matthews had them. How did she know about that? But she knew everything. New York! Sue had never been to New York. Now she was going to work there! It was too marvellous!

There was only one fly in the ointment – Kit and Connie. But that was two flies, Sue thought, and laughed aloud at her own idiocy, so that a probationer, coming along the corridor, stared at her with alarmed eyes. All the same, it would be *awful* to be without the girls – the three of them had been together so long. Now it would all have to end. Connie was going to marry Phil, and Kit wouldn't be interested in Public Health work – she wanted to do institutional work of some kind. She was wearing a staff nurse's band already, in the Amphitheatre, and she'd either remain there or go to some other hospital.

What would the girls think of this new plan?

She told them that evening.

Sue had 'last hours' off duty, and Kit and Connie had come over early from supper. They were all three curled up on the long couch in the living-room of Grafton Hall. When they arrived in the living-room, Grafton had been silent except for their own voices, an occasional creak from the elevator, or a distant step. Now, and all at once, came the sound of laughter, shrieks, steps running in the corridors, uniforms rustling on the stairs, the elevator rattling upward with a load of voices. The day nurses were off duty.

Sue listened to the familiar sounds with a little half-smile curving her lips. How alive the place was!

'And so,' Sue finished her account, 'she said I ought to go to Henry Street.'

Kit was sprawled back against the cushions, her cap over one ear. 'I think it's a swell idea,' she said. 'New York would be fun, and the work is just the kind of thing to suit you. You'd love it, Sue.'

'I know I would. It's –'

'Girls! Girls!' Hilda Grayson surged through the big double doors. She was breathless with excitement. 'Girls! What do you think! Miss Matthews has offered me a job as head nurse in the Children's Medical Out-Patient! Isn't it marvellous? I never dreamed –'

There was a chorus of congratulations.

'Are any of the rest of you staying on?' Hilda asked wistfully, when the enthusiasm had subsided a little. 'I know Connie's getting married. But what about –'

'I'm going to Henry Street Settlement,' Sue said.

'*Henry Street!* Oooh!' Hilda stared. 'Gosh, Bat, I'd be scared stiff to do that!'

'Sit down, Hilda,' Kit said. 'Stiffen if you must – but not on my feet.'

Hilda sat down, automatically obedient to any order.

'Why would you be scared, Hilda? Sue asked.

'Why – oh – because – well, look where you have to go – way off there in the slums of New York – and it's simply crawling with gangsters and murderers and goodness knows what! Why, if a murderer came up to me and said, "Follow me," I'd – I'd –'

The girls shouted with laughter.

'Hilda!' Sue gasped. 'Where do you get such ghoulish ideas? Honestly!'

'But it's – I mean – it *is* awfully scary around those slums.'

'Not for a nurse, it isn't,' Sue said quietly.

'But all kinds of things happen – and you'll have to live there! Why, I wouldn't –'

'I would,' Kit said, not looking at Sue.

'Oh dear! Are *you* going too? There won't be anybody left –'

'I'm going if they'll take me – and Bat would like to have me.'

Sue's feet hit the floor. She was up in one bound.

'Kitty! Do you *mean* it? I thought you wanted to be – will you *really* go with me? Oh, Kit! How perfect!'

The undemonstrative Kit flushed painfully. 'Public Health work is a good thing to know about,' she said. 'Besides, somebody will have to protect you from

Hilda's murderer – not to mention the gangsters and other suspicious characters. I shall see that you never go out without a large cannon and an axe. I'll carry the machine gun, and Connie can –' She stopped.

They looked at Connie, who, all this time, had been sitting quietly on the couch saying nothing whatever and glancing from Sue to Kit with suspiciously bright eyes. Connie wouldn't be with them. Connie was getting married.

There was a silence.

'What's all this?' said Lois Wilmont's voice behind them. 'Are you playing Quaker Meeting, or what?' She was actually facetious.

'Willie,' said Sue, 'you're frivolous! Something's happened! You look as if you were stuffed with cream puffs!'

'I've got a job!' Willie announced.

'The word is "situation," Willie,' Kit grinned.

'Where?' Sue cried.

Willie beamed upon them from heights of glory. 'I'm going to be assistant night supervisor – right here,' she said.

'Willie! How marvellous!' Connie cried warmly, finding her voice at last.

'You'll blow the top right off the hospital night life,' Kit said.

'Do we have to stand up when you come into a room?' Hilda asked, awed.

Sue dropped to her knees, and the other three followed suit, kneeling in a solemn row at the feet of the happy Willie, who flushed, and laughed, and said they were idiots. She was, as Sue remarked later, 'practically human for the first, and probably the last, time in her life.'

There was other news. Ted Hanscom was going to be instructor in practical nursing in a little new training school. Grace Holton was going to be a dentist's assistant. Francesca Manson was going to Labrador with the Grenfell expedition.

'And a good place for her,' Kit said grimly. 'She ought to be in a cold place. It's her natural habitat.'

'Girls,' Willie said, still flushed with her new honour, 'do you realise that graduation is a week from to-night?'

'We had that impression,' said Kit. 'You ought to march a couple of paces in front of the rest of us, Willie. If you don't, nobody'll know that you're practically a supervisor already.'

'It's going to be awfully strange,' Connie said suddenly, 'not belonging here any more – not to see these old corridors – not to –'

'You give me the creeps,' Kit put in hastily. 'Who wants a spot of ice-cream?'

Everybody wanted ice-cream.

Kit, in a sudden fit of nobility, offered to go out and get it for them, and in the general stir all thoughts of leaving the hospital were safely turned aside.

That night, however, before Sue went to bed, she opened her top bureau drawer and took out a glove box. Inside it lay a card, around which was wrapped an inch-wide band of black velvet. The card read:

> *To be worn three years from now!*
> *Congratulations.*
> E.M. Waring

Sue's throat tightened. How terrified she'd been that day – the day she got her cap, and had come off duty to find this on her dresser. Was it only two and a half years ago? It seemed longer – so much had happened since. And now, in a few days, it would be her right to wear that band on her cap. She would have to take it off again, but only for a while. And after that – Henry Street, with Kit!

Everything was such fun, even though Bill – her thoughts faltered, and for a moment the old pain returned, a dull, heavy ache in her chest. But she'd learned about that now. It came, it vanished, and one went on as before. If it were still there, underneath, at least it no longer frightened her.

17
Graduation

Commencement exercises were to begin at eight-thirty.

Sue dressed early, in fresh grey uniform – with long sleeves, for it was autumn now; spotless apron; bib, collar, and cuffs shining and hard with starch. Her new cap lay on the dresser with the band around it, sharply black above the tiny white ruffle.

Sue looked at it and swallowed.

Then she set the cap on her head, and stared incredulous at her image in the mirror. She scarcely saw the slender figure, immaculate in grey and white. There was only that black curve above the bronze-gold sheen of her hair – a velvet circle of years.

Hard work and ceaseless effort had put it there.

A diploma was a piece of parchment with words written on it – something to put away in a trunk and produce only if one were asked to do so. But the proud black band was there on the cap for anyone to see.

She turned away at last and went slowly out and down the corridor.

Dad and Mother were coming on a late train. Ted, Mother wrote, couldn't leave school in the middle of the week. Sue wouldn't be able to meet them. They would arrive just before the exercises began, and she would have to be with her class by that time.

Mother, Sue thought, would be proud and happy because she loved Sue. Dad would also be proud because he loved her – but he would understand better. He was a doctor. He knew what this meant.

Sue avoided the elevator and hurried past the floor landings. She didn't want to go into rooms and talk. She wanted to be by herself for a little while – to get quiet inside.

The stairs leading to the basement had a water-tank on the first landing. Sue's mouth was dry with excitement. She went down the three steps and filled a paper cup with water, drinking slowly, and grinning up at the maid who had come to the head of the stairs to cry:

'Oh, lookit Miss Barton with her black band on!'

The doorbell rang, and the maid vanished.

Sue dropped her paper cup in the container and ran lightly down the stairs. She didn't hear the maid calling after her. She wanted to wander around in the warm, dimly lighted basement and feel all the hospital – her hospital – going on over her head. Nobody would bother her in the basement.

There were steps behind her, but she was absorbed in her own thoughts and did not hear them.

The basement entrance to Orthopedic loomed before her. The three months there had been fun, in spite of aching back and tired feet. She smiled, remembering the Italian patient, Mrs Riccino, and her miracle – and funny little Sophie Wenesky, the mischief maker.

She must be under the X-ray rooms now. The first thing she'd ever done in the hospital had been to take a patient to X-ray.

That muffled tramping overhead would be in the big brick corridor. It was a lovely old place, vast, high-ceilinged, warmly red, always smelling of soap-suds. Sunlight lay in great pools on the floor. It was from there, on Christmas Eve, two years before, that she had watched Miss Cameron standing in the falling snow, listening to the carol singers – and had realized what that grim and splendid woman had done for the school.

Sue turned suddenly to look over her shoulder, thinking that she heard someone behind her. There was no one in sight.

She moved on slowly among the crackling steam pipes, scarcely noticing where her feet were taking her until she passed a lighted doorway and, glancing beyond it, saw a pile of bulging laundry bags waiting to be collected by Tony.

It was somewhere along here that she had been lost, her first day in the hospital. She smiled, re-membering how Tony had frightened her. Bill had found her at last, and had shown her the way out. It must have been right here that he found her. She'd been sitting –

'*Sue!*' said a voice.

Sue whirled, the colour draining from her face.

He came directly to her, his tall figure and dark head indistinct in the gloom. It was as though a trapdoor had opened beneath Sue's feet.

'Why – Bill!' she managed to say, and tried to smile at him – tried to be bright and casual – tried to be that nice little girl he used to know. Her voice said stupidly, 'Where – did *you* come from?'

He took her hand in both of his, holding it,

imprisoned. 'I've come from New Hampshire,' he said, as Sue had said three years before in this same place.

There was constraint in their remembering laughter. Sue laid her other hand on the warm asbestos of a steam pipe, clinging to it to steady the sudden trembling of her knees.

'I hope,' she said, 'that you haven't come all the way from New Hampshire without your dinner.'

He laughed, not quite naturally. 'That wasn't what came next,' he said. 'You demanded very rudely to be told what time it was.'

'Oh yes!' Sue leaned against the pipe. 'W-what *are* you doing here, Bill?'

He still retained her hand. 'I've come to your graduation,' he said. 'Aren't you glad to see me?'

He had come to her graduation! He hadn't come to see Gerard!

'*Are* you glad to see me?' he asked again.

'Wild horses,' Sue said, 'wouldn't drag such an admission from me. It would be unmaidenly.' She couldn't turn her eyes from his, or stop the rising tide of tenderness that closed her throat and misted her eyes.

He saw, then, and caught his breath, lifting her hand to his cheek, to hold it there.

'Very proper and demure,' he said. 'Tell me, Miss Barton – Sue – if I may call you that –' He faltered; then, still with forced lightness – 'Dare I ask you again for your hand in marriage?'

Sue's other hand clenched against the pipe.

'I fear, Dr Barry, that you have surprised my little secret. Oh, Bill – I love you awfully – and I've missed you so! It's been – horrible!'

'Then you *will* marry me?'

'Yes.'

His arms were around her, his lips on hers.

Sue disengaged herself at last, looking up at him, wordless and shaken. He saw the black band on her cap and put up his hand to touch it.

She laughed tremulously. 'Bill,' she said at last, 'please don't think I'm green-eyed and seething, or about to break off this pipe and hit you with it – but I *have* to know – what about Eleanor Gerard?'

'Eleanor Gerard?' He stared at her.

She told him all that Francesca had said – and seen.

His face cleared. 'Oh!' he said. 'Why, I went to the theatre with the Brownlows, and saw her in the lobby. I stopped to speak to her and she put her hand through my arm. We walked to the door, talking.' He grinned boyish. 'I don't believe that's enough to compromise me, do you?'

Sue had listened in a dazed silence.

'But then you didn't write,' she said weakly.

'I didn't want to nag at you. I thought if you were quite free of me for a while – girl doesn't hear from boy – absence makes the heart grow fonder, and all that –'

'*Oh!* Oh, *Bill* – you *idiot!*'

'Then it's all right?'

'Yes. It's over now.' She drew a long and thankful breath. 'Let's not think about it. But you *might* tell me what you've been doing all this time.' She rested folded arms on the dusty pipe and laid her flushed cheek on them. 'Even if I do love you,' she added, 'I haven't got second sight.'

'I'm going to be a country doctor,' he said. 'Do you

mind? There was an opening in Springdale. The only doctor there is getting old – he was in college with my father – and Dad wrote me, so I went up. I wasn't sure how it would turn out. I wasn't even sure you'd be interested, so I didn't –'

'I think,' said Sue sweetly, 'that I *will* break off this pipe and hit you with it! Oh, Bill, how *could* you be such a lunatic? We – we were supposed to be – friends – at least – and – Oh, Bill – I'm *glad* you're going to be a country doctor! They're so marvellous!'

'*Are* you glad?' His arms came around her again, his eyes shining with relief.

It was on the way back through the dim passage-ways to the stairs that led to the big brick corridor that Bill said suddenly, 'Now that I've got you – would it be impertinent to inquire *when* you're going to marry me?'

Sue paused abruptly.

'Bill,' she said, 'I have to explain something. Please, *please* understand, and don't be hurt. I – I'm terribly – in love with you. But – could I – please – not get married just yet? I've hardly – begun – to do things. I've wanted so much to be a nurse, and I've worked so hard. I know, as your wife, I can still be a nurse if I want to – but *not on my own!* That's terribly important to me, Bill. I want to go to Henry Street. I want to do things for a while – first – by myself. I – I'd rather not even tell anyone that we're engaged – just yet. It is – too much – to ask?'

He was silent for a long moment, his eyes wistful on her lovely young face. Then he straightened up, smiling.

'You wouldn't be you if you didn't want to be

independent, Sue dear. I – it's one of the reasons I love you.' He drew a long breath. 'Do whatever you wish,' he said. 'When you're ready – let me know. Your father said –'

'*Dad?*'

'Yes. I called on your family last summer. I told your father then. I – think he likes me. But he said that I'd have to give you – your own, redheaded way.'

'Bill dear! I won't make it too long,' Sue said bravely, and lifting both arms she drew his head down and kissed him – it was a seal and a promise.

The big brick corridor was loud with the voices of seventy-two girls. They were forming a double line already – a double line of white caps and black bands. There was Willie, stiff and complacent; Hilda, round-eyed and out of breath; Grace Holton, shrieking; Kit, Connie, Francesca –

Sue hurried along the line. What would they say if they *knew*? But they weren't going to know. It would be her secret for a while, hers and Bill's – and Dad's and Mother's, of course. But no one else – not even Kit and Connie. She'd tell them a little later – but not now.

'Right here, Miss Barton!' Miss Mason called, and Sue stepped into the grey and white ranks.

There was constant stirring in the double line – nurses turning to look – calling out. Their words were flippant – their voices tremulous. They looked at the big brick corridor with eyes already homesick for it, and called it 'this dump.' They touched the bands on their caps with reverent fingers and said that wearing it for one night didn't mean a thing – it was a lot of hooey! They swallowed lumps in their throats and said they'd be glad to get out of here – if they ever did.

The rest of the school was gathering now, falling into line behind the double row of black bands – the intermediate and junior nurses, then the blue ranks of the probationers. An embarrassed house officer hastened through the corridor to be mocked with the rhythmic tramping of several hundred pairs of feet.

Miss Mason held up her hand at last, for silence, and the babble died away to a murmur. It was almost time to start.

Suddenly, as though pulled by one string, the capped heads turned to the rear. There was a hush.

Through the door at the far end of the corridor – the door from Brewster – came an austere white figure with a familiar bounding walk.

Miss Cameron swept along the line, her eyes critical on the assembled uniforms. She was smiling a little.

A ripple of applause started, followed her, grew in volume, swelled to a roaring beat, until the great corridor trembled with the steady, rocking vibration – the spontaneous tribute of all the school to a great women, a great teacher, a great nurse.

Sue caught a glimmer of tears in Miss Cameron's eyes as the commanding figure strode past to the rotunda.

The line began to move, slowly at first, then with a tramping shuffle down the old corridor, over the worn floors, and out at last into a blazing circle of light and row upon row of faces. The graduating class filed through to their places and the school fell in behind them.

Sue looked hastily at the blue of faces before she sat down.

There they were! Dad and Mother – and beside them, Bill! Three pairs of eyes shone watching Sue, looking at her slenderness, proud in the grey uniform; at the delicate face, flushed with happiness. Mother's eyes saw only her baby girl. But Bill and Dad saw the black band above the red curls – the brave black band of achievement.

The graduating class sat down.

Miss Matthews rose and came to the front of the platform that faced the audience, and began to speak.

All graduation exercises are alike. Sue listened without hearing. All this was for fathers and mothers and friends. A distinguished guest speaker took Miss Matthews's place and droned the conventional phrases – 'going out into the world . . . noble profession . . . as I look at these young faces . . . humanity will long' . . . and so forth, and so forth.

There was music.

Sue heard her name called and went up to receive her diploma. This wasn't the real graduation. The real graduation had been back there in the big brick corridor when the class, in that thunder of applause, had said good-bye to Miss Cameron and all that she stood for in the school.

Everything was over at last and the crowd straggled across to Grafton Hall for the dancing.

Dad and Mother were taking the night train back. Sue went out with them to stand on the front steps. She told them, then, about Bill.

'I thought that would happen, dear,' Mother said, her eyes filling. 'We – we like him so much.'

Dad grinned under his moustache.

'He's a nice chap – but don't hurry, kid. Show the world what you can do before you settle down.'

'I shall,' Sue promised.

She stood where they left her, feeling the autumn air cool on her face. From somewhere, far over distant hills, came a faint smell of burning leaves. The lights of the hospital were points of gold in the darkness.

The door opened behind her. Sue knew, without turning, that it was Bill.

They stood side by wide, not speaking, looking at the hospital they loved; at the winking lights of the wards; at the roofs above them, massed black against the sky. The wind whispered in the elm leaves and stirred the ivy clinging to red brick and granite. Far down the street an ambulance gong clamoured for right of way in its race to the hospital – to young doctors and young nurses.

'And they'll be ready – just as we are ready,' Bill said.

Other great reads ⌐ from **Red Fox**

Further Red Fox titles that you might enjoy reading are listed on the following pages. They are available in bookshops or they can be ordered directly from us.

If you would like to order books, please send this form and the money due to:

ARROW BOOKS, BOOKSERVICE BY POST, PO BOX 29, DOUGLAS, ISLE OF MAN, BRITISH ISLES. Please enclose a cheque or postal order made out to Arrow Books Ltd for the amount due, plus 30p per book for postage and packing to a maximum of £3.00, both for orders within the UK. For customers outside the UK, please allow 35p per book.

NAME _____

ADDRESS _____

_____

Please print clearly.

Whilst every effort is made to keep prices low, it is sometimes necessary to increase cover prices at short notice. If you are ordering books by post, to save delay it is advisable to phone to confirm the correct price. The number to ring is THE SALES DEPARTMENT 071 (if outside London) 973 9700.

Other great reads from **Red Fox**

Enter the gripping world of the REDWALL saga

REDWALL   Brian Jacques

It is the start of the summer of the Late Rose. Redwall Abbey, the peaceful home of a community of mice, slumbers in the warmth of a summer afternoon. The mice are preparing for a great jubilee feast.

But not for long. Cluny is coming! The evil one-eyed rat warlord is advancing with his battle-scarred mob. And Cluny wants Redwall . . .

ISBN 0 09 951200 9   £3.50

MOSSFLOWER   Brian Jacques

One late autumn evening, Bella of Brockhall snuggled deep in her armchair and told a story . . .

This is the dramatic tale behind the bestselling *Redwall*. It is the gripping account of how Redwall Abbey was founded through the bravery of the legendary mouse Martin and his epic quest for Salmandastron. Once again, the forces of good and evil are at war in a stunning novel that will captivate readers of all ages.

ISBN 0 09 955400 3   £3.50

MATTIMEO   Brian Jacques

Slagar the fox is intent on revenge . . .

On bringing death and destruction to the inhabitants of Redwall Abbey, in particular to the fearless warrior mouse Matthias. Gathering his evil band around him, Slagar plots to strike at the heart of the Abbey. His cunning and cowardly plan is to steal the Redwall children—and Mattimeo, Matthias' son, is to be the biggest prize of all.

ISBN 0 09 967540 4   £3.50

Other great reads ⌇ *from* **Red Fox**

THE WINTER VISITOR   Joan Lingard

Strangers didn't come to Nick Murray's home town in winter.
And they didn't lodge at his house. But Ed Black had—and Nick
Murray didn't like it.

Why had Ed come? The small Scottish seaside resort was
bleak, cold and grey at that time of year. The answer, Nick
begins to suspect, lies with his mother—was there some past
connection between her and Ed?

ISBN 0 09 938590 2   £1.99

STRANGERS IN THE HOUSE   Joan Lingard

Calum resents his mother remarrying. He doesn't want to move
to a flat in Edinburgh with a new father and a thirteen-year-old
stepsister. Stella, too, dreads the new marriage. Used to living
alone with her father she loathes the idea of sharing their small
flat.

Stella's and Calum's struggles to adapt to a new life, while
trying to cope with the problems of growing up are related with
great poignancy in a book which will be enjoyed by all older
readers.

ISBN 0 09 955020 2   £1.95

Other great reads ✎ *from* **Red Fox**

Discover the great animal stories of Colin Dann

JUST NUFFIN

The Summer holidays loomed ahead with nothing to look forward to except one dreary week in a caravan with only Mum and Dad for company. Roger was sure he'd be bored.

But then Dad finds Nuffin: an abandoned puppy who's more a bundle of skin and bones than a dog. Roger's holiday is transformed and he and Nuffin are inseparable. But Dad is adamant that Nuffin must find a new home. Is there *any* way Roger can persuade him to change his mind?

ISBN 0 09 966900 5   £2.99

KING OF THE VAGABONDS

'You're very young,' Sammy's mother said, 'so heed my advice. Don't go into Quartermile Field.'

His mother and sister are happily domesticated but Sammy, the tabby cat, feels different. They are content with their lot, never wondering what lies beyond their immediate surroundings. But Sammy is burningly curious and his life seems full of mysteries. Who is his father? Where has he gone? And what is the mystery of Quartermile Field?

ISBN 0 09 957190 0   £2.50

Other great reads *from* **Red Fox**

Haunting fiction for older readers from Red Fox

THE XANADU MANUSCRIPT
John Rowe Townsend

There is nothing unusual about visitors in Cambridge.

So what is it about three tall strangers which fills John with a mixture of curiosity and unease? Not only are they strikingly handsome but, for apparently educated people, they are oddly surprised and excited by normal, everyday events. And, as John pursues them, their mystery only seems to deepen.

Set against a background of an old university town, this powerfully compelling story is both utterly fantastic and oddly convincing.

'An author from whom much is expected and received.' *Economist*

ISBN 0 09 9751801 £2.50

ONLOOKER Roger Davenport

Peter has always enjoyed being in Culver Wood, and dismissed the tales of hauntings, witchcraft and superstitions associated with it. But when he starts having extraordinary visions that are somehow connected with the wood, and which become more real to him than his everyday life, he realizes that something is taking control of his mind in an inexplicable and frightening way.

Through his uneasy relationship with Isobel and her father, a Professor of Archaeology interested in excavating Culver Wood, Peter is led to the discovery of the wood's secret and his own terrifying part in it.

ISBN 0 09 9750708 £2.50

*Other great reads from **Red Fox***

AMAZING ORIGAMI FOR CHILDREN
Steve and Megumi Biddle

Origami is an exciting and easy way to make toys, decorations and all kinds of useful things from folded paper.

Use leftover gift paper to make a party hat and a fancy box. Or create a colourful lorry, a pretty rose and a zoo full of origami animals. There are over 50 fun projects in Amazing Origami.

Following Steve and Megumi's step-by-step instructions and clear drawings, you'll amaze your friends and family with your magical paper creations.

ISBN 0 09 9661802   £4.99

MAGICAL STRING   Steve and Megumi Biddle

With only a loop of string you can make all kinds of shapes, puzzles and games. Steve and Megumi Biddle provide all the instructions and diagrams that are needed to create their amazing string magic in another of their inventive and absorbing books.

ISBN 0 09 964470 3   £2.50